MARIE MCGANN

The Drawbridge

BRANDON

A Brandon Original Paperback

This edition published in 2001 by
Brandon
an imprint of Mount Eagle Publications
Dingle, Co. Kerry, Ireland

10 9 8 7 6 5 4 3 2 1

Copyright © Marie McGann 2001

The author has asserted her moral rights

ISBN 0 86322 271 4
(original paperback)

The verses on pages 96–7 are from
"Wild Mountain Thyme" © J. McPeake

This book is published with the assistance of
the Arts Council/An Chomhairle Ealaíonn

Cover design: id communications, Tralee
Typesetting by Red Barn Publishing, Skeagh, Skibbereen
Printed by ColourBooks, Dublin

To my people,
the Kellys and McGanns of East Galway

Chapter One

THE DESERTIONS

Some women take years to accept a husband's sudden disappearance, some the rest of their lives, some a day, beginning to feel more themselves by the minute. I took five days. My husband Stanley was gone. Gone where? Nobody knew. Gone why? Nobody could tell. He had absconded without trace like snow in high summer, and not as in just gone fishing. He had abandoned me and our son Malachy in that big house. Mind you, I should have been forewarned when he failed to arrive home for roast veal and orange stuffing on our sixteenth wedding anniversary. He was punctilious about family occasions and in our years together had only missed Malachy's twelfth birthday party because a patient had set fire to the clinic curtains. You could not watch them all the time. I had often wished that Stanley had chosen a less harrowing if less hallowed branch of medicine, like geriatrics for instance, where the patients were going to die no matter what you did to them, but then he did like a challenge. I put the dried-up remains of the dinner on Fred's plate and went to bed prepared to tell Stanley the dinner was in the dog, but never did get the chance.

I rang his nurse in the morning, but the woman knew nothing except that the waiting room was full of disturbed patients getting more disturbed by the minute. She sounded fretful, cross. One of the hazards of the job, I thought kindly, and immediately became fretful and cross myself. When Stanley did not come on the second night, I had to face the thought of calling the police. In case of an accident. It was getting difficult to avoid Malachy's questions.

"Where's Dad, Mimmo?"

"Staying with friends in town, I guess."

"He never does that, Mom."

"There's always a first time for everything."

I would have to swallow my pride and call the police, imagining the winks, the nudges. No wonder Dr Finucane had hightailed it. Red-haired women were devils to live with, and an Irish one to boot. But when I did call, they were kind, concerned. I could leave it with them. They would check it out and report back. But there was not a dickybird to report. No accidents, no deaths. I chain-smoked, drank too much whiskey, stayed within earshot of the telephone. Hurt pride forbade me to tell anyone, not even Zofia Mirska at the Polish delicatessen, who was always a rock in a crisis. If there was any leaving to be done, I would have wanted to do it. The thought that my man had beaten me to it weighed lump-ishly on my humiliated rebellious soul. Malachy came and lay beside me one night.

"If he was dead they'd have found him by now, Mom."

"Don't talk like that, Malachy."

"He could have amnesia."

"We must wait and see."

"Mom, you gotta cut down on the drinking and the smoking."

He put an arm around me and later I heard him crying into the pillow.

But it was not amnesia, or if it was he had felt it coming on. The mortgage was paid off and there was £50,000 in the bank in my name. Then I knew. I went numb and smiled my widest at the cashier as if there was nothing unusual about that, and walked home, smiling as I had done for years to cover the secret knowledge lurking inside me that happiness was for others. I would have to tell Tom and Lydia Jones next door. I had promised to mind their small son, Disraeli, if Lydia's mother grew weaker or died in Jamaica. I walked, head erect, past the library and the stone lady sculpted by Huxley Jones (whose widow had married a bishop) and locked myself into the bathroom with a half bottle of bourbon, letting the taps run to drown the sound of my sobs of rage. It wasn't the first time somebody had left me without warning, but this time it was wounded pride, not grief, which was stunning me first.

I was not yet four when I first attended the village school. My mother Mary Rafferty said it was a relief. I believe that from the time I had first walked I had tried to follow my brother everywhere and had screamed so loudly when prevented that Mary put cotton wool in her ears to get on with the house work.

"Be grateful there is nothing wrong with her lungs," said my grandmother Delia on a rare visit to her daughter-in-law.

My father, the quiet John Rafferty, taught physics in the nearby town and escaped this morning uproar. In the end, Mrs Twibill, the headmistress, agreed to see how I got on. Mary stood at the gate with Delia as I crossed the market place holding Shane's hand. My new rain-cape and satchel were too big for me, and my mother Mary Rafferty was afraid the neighbours would notice. I didn't care about the neighbours.

"She is very stubborn and noisy for three," I heard Mary say.

"She is as hardy as a mountain goat," said Delia, "the image of her grandfather Ferdinand, red mane and all, and I can tell you after forty years of marriage that there is no holding the likes of them back. Best not to wait too long for the next child."

But there was no other child for Mary and John, and people said that I was the shakings of the bag. Mary said that the school wouldn't keep me, but she was wrong. Mrs Twibill said it would be easier for everyone if Brigid Mary Rafferty, Brid for short, began her schooling. That was me. I had a wonderful time with chalk, a blackboard and an ink pot in the infant class, and dusk had won the day when we got home. I forgot the raincoat, spilled ink on my legs, got wet, and nobody said a cross word to me.

Summer was spent with Delia and Ferdinand on the farm, deep in the countryside. I loved to come down with Delia in the morning to flex my bare feet on the flagstones, let the sheepdogs curl around and kiss my legs, making no sound or they would be put out. I never made a move to go with Shane and Ferdy to the fields on the reaper and binder. My place was with Delia. I learned to pluck the feathers off dead chickens and could wander freely about the farm, as long as I stayed away from the horses' legs.

"The goats don't think it's dangerous. They suck the horses' tails and don't get kicked," I said.

"The horses know the goats are young and have no sense," said Delia, busy with the churning.

"I am young," I said.

"The horses expect you to have more wisdom than a goat," said Delia, swinging the heavy milk barrel. "The Lord gives them their wisdom as He gives you yours."

"I haven't much wisdom," I said.

"You have enough. An old head on young shoulders is not in God's plan and brings a curse with it."

I was in charge of shooing the horses from eating the bracken, for it destroyed their vitamin D, but I never went near their legs again. Delia could get me to do anything she asked. I loved to watch the milk change to buttermilk and then to yellow butter. Buttermilk kept cold in earthenware pitchers covered with muslin was the best thirst quencher for the parched men in from the fields. The Poles reintroduced me to buttermilk thirty years later, but the magic was gone. Refrigeration was not the same, as perhaps nothing was ever the same again without Delia. Did I never get over the loss of Delia, even if her peaceful death did not come without warning? I did not. Does anyone ever get over anything, even if the world seems full of merry widows? Like everyone else, I got on with life, dragging out the less painful memories from time to time to keep me going, but life could not be the same. Like the smell and taste of water drawn from the well by roped buckets could never be the same anywhere else. Like going to the well through the fields of clover, down the rutted track past the peaceful sheep and lambs, and the finger-sucking calves could never be the wonder of the world without Delia. Everything on the farm was alive for Shane and me, even the silence in the granary loft, filled with grain for the spring scattering, or the stables with horses sleeping on the straw. Or the sounds of the flute, the violin or the accordion around the fire at night, where the cooking pots hung on irons over the flames and soda bread baked on a griddle. The sound of that wistful reckless music of my childhood could, years later in a London pub or the Underground, transfix me for days with grief too deep for words. It is foolish to ask if I ever got over the loss of my country.

Separation from the grandparents was eased by the excitement of being back in the village of Kilcuan on a fair day, with lowing cows in pens and farmers thronging the market place, settling prices, splitting the difference with a spit on the palm and a slap of the hand. To be back in time for the pilgrimage to St Cuan's Well, dating from 788AD, and to lie listening to the croaking of the frogs in the long grass by the river. That was the time when the sluice gates were closed at the weir, and the water, green and stagnant around the bulrushes, trickled under the gates to where the little children paddled. That was the time that was good for the farmers and everyone else, even Mary Rafferty, who got a rest from us children being under her feet all day. It was different in the wintertime when the rains closed in on the village, thundering on the slate and thatched roofs, blinding the windows, driving the light from the sky so that John lit the oil lamps during the day. Doors were shut and windows shuttered until the rain stopped and strong winds dried the steaming roofs and streaming pavements. After the rains the cocks crew in celebration, dogs excited by new smells barked, and the slow hiss of the ganders sounded in the backyards. I could tell the passing of the rainstorms by the lazy dripping, striking a tonic sol-fa on the galvanised roof outside the bedroom window. Delia said that some things in life were hard, like having babies and going away to convents where Shane could not go, and best to accept them. You had to do something secret to have a baby, and Shane said you couldn't catch anybody doing it for it was a mortal sin unless you were married, when you had to do it whether you liked it or not, because it was a sin not to have lots of children. Neither Shane nor I knew where God was, although Mary said that He was at the wheel of Father Flynn's car, as he never had an accident driving on the wrong side of the road for thirty years. Mary drove into a stationary lorry the first time John tried to teach her to drive. He thought she was not suited by temperament to drive, and she said it suited him to think so and she would drive if she liked, but she never did.

They did send me away to the convent. The train travelled miles across desolate fields and dusty railway stations until it reached the destination at the foot of the mountains. The nuns looked like penguins on skates with their heads encased in white starched boxes with the underside missing for the chin. I liked the smell of burning candles in the chapel and the red lamp at the golden box where Christ was kept. Churches without the red light were always to make me feel sad and empty. The family came to visit me on Parents' Day. John said I had got tall, Mary said I was pale, and Shane said nothing. When I wrote asking them not to come any more, Mary was offended by the strange letter from her strange daughter, but John said the visit had heightened my loneliness and I would grow out of it. For once he was wrong. I did not grow out of it. Shane knew that and never came again. It was too hard on us both.

The holidays approached when we would all go home except for the nuns, who would never go home again. I was in a frenzy of interior excitement, thinking how they would all be at the railway station to meet me. Mother Genevieve told me gently in her soft sibilant voice that Shane had had an accident, had been knocked off his bicycle, and she would send me to the railway station in a taxi. The train journey was a nightmare of anxiety, and when I got to the home station, I could tell at once by the faces that there was no need to ask how he was. They brought me to the chapel where he lay in the flower-laden coffin in barbaric repose, the side of his face disfigured with a port wine stain, the light extinguished, gone for ever from behind the closed lids. I was told to accept the loss, to grieve, but I knew better, for while I did not want to live without him, neither could I withstand such pain. So eventually I began to eat again. I blocked it off, pulling up a drawbridge in my mind, and never willingly spoke of my brother for years. To anybody. Not even to my father. More especially to my father, with his faith in God's plan. I withdrew, and I never got over it, because I refused to accept it. My reaction to Stanley's disappearance had more to do with wounded pride and monumental rage than the breaking of a heart already broken and left behind in Ireland.

Chapter Two

THE HUSBAND

I first saw Stanley Finucane in a creased white coat, stethoscope hanging out of his pocket, walking silently on rubber soled shoes into the pool of light at the end of the hospital ward. Dolores Kelly and I were new student nurses, fearful of every sound on the male surgical ward, the snoring, the swearing, the creaking of traction pulleys, even the tinkling of the beaded water jug covers. He asked for the sphygmomanometer, but neither Kelly nor I could pronounce it, never mind find it for him. Surely, we were not in charge of this ward, where experience could make the difference between life and death, the young doctor said, but I assured him that the night sister was in the office next door. Stanley smiled and went up the ward shining his torch on the intravenous drips. Kelly said she would love a night of sin with him, but she was not prepared to stand in a queue. I could understand the queue. He was tall, broad shouldered, squarish in a dependable sort of way, with springy black hair and black lashes around quiet grey eyes unusual in an Irishman. A cleft chin did his appearance no harm. Dolores said he came from west of the river Shannon like me, and I looked forward to meeting him again, but we were both dismissed after two months as being unfit to nurse the sick.

We had got off to a bad start, unable to keep the required low profile with Dolores' height and my unruly red hair. In the first week I had walked past the matron's table in the dining room wearing a bloodstained apron I had not made time to change and forfeited my week's leave there and then. I said I had no time, and the matron said I must learn to make it. She looked to me like an affronted camel with her lofty, aggressive, half-lidded gaze. Dolores was the next to be caught, smoking a Woodbine cigarette as we soaked aching feet in basins of hot water. Gifted as I was with acute hearing, I had time to fling my water and cigarette out the window, but Dolores, who talked too much, had not. For punishment we found ourselves on night duty on a surgical male ward. We saw it as a bonus. Men patients were easier than women, who needed bedpans and had more things on their lockers to dust. You could fling a urinal to a man while on the run down the ward to some fearsome crisis. Mind you, you had to learn to handle the gropers and the flashers in the lavatories, even if you got more presents from them. During the day we learned to climb out of the sleeping quarters without tearing stockings on the rusty fire escape. We got away with it until the Elvis Presley matinee, when we found ourselves sitting beside the matron and her male companion as the lights went up in the cinema. I thought the woman would be too ashamed to be seen in the cheap seats with a man in the daytime to confront us. Dolores also thought she would not have the nerve to admit she saw us, never mind sack us, but she had and she did, and really it was as well before one of us killed someone. We had lasted two months. My mother Mary Rafferty had given me three weeks, and my father John had said it was as well to get it out of my system while I was young enough to further my education, so they were neither too shocked nor surprised.

Within the year I enrolled in the Dublin National University for the dental course. It paid better and sooner than medicine, and the ghastly dissection of the formaldehyde corpses was confined to the head, neck and shoulders, avoiding the abdomen and the private parts. I was in my twenties when I saw Stanley again, as I sat nursing a glass of strong cider and an angry heart at a medical dance in the Aula Maxima.

"Mindless sheep," my admirer from Harrogate had said as the people streamed into St Patrick's Cathedral.

"A syphilitic wife murderer started your religion," I had said crossly, fraught from forcing metallurgy into my head.

"At least we are not drunk seven nights a week."

"It's more fun than washing your bloody cars on Sundays."

We had stared helplessly at each other, and I had not looked back as I walked away. So much for Anglo-Irish relationships.

"Do you mind if I sit here?"

I did not look up or reply.

"Have we not met before?"

How unoriginal, I thought, but I did look up and it was him. There was no mistaking the light grey eyes and the cleft chin. I danced with him all night, and the rock and roll music took my mind off my insulted heart. I gave him my telephone number when the dance was over, but he never rang, and after a few weeks I put it to the back of my mind and tackled materia medica instead. I was tired of men. Such unaccustomed diligence did not pass unnoticed, and I became known as the Amalgam Queen, bestowed with friendly derision by the rest of the final year students. Being the only girl among thirty dental students, though a matter of envy to some, brought few rewards with it. I was treated as one of the boys, as likely as any of them to mishaps with hot wax, soldering metal, ruined exposed cavities and loss of conservable teeth. I was as prone as any of the men to failed anaesthetics, to formocresol burned tongues, a matter of litigation if discovered, to the horrors of belligerent adult patients and screaming restless children. I battled through, strained to the limits of my energy, and passed the final examinations, ossified, as was the popular term, bone stiff with fear.

"How will you stand kids in the chair?" they asked me, as I had decided I would make dentures for nobody.

"How will you stand adults?" I retorted.

None of us knew whether we could stand dentistry at all. Though we were all in it for the money, we feared that groping around in the oral cavity, while preferable to other orifices, was going to be very taxing. As I did not like the thought of making dentures for the rest of my life, I decided that working with children and preventative dentistry was the best escape. As soon as I went to England I trained to advanced level of hypnotherapy in Cambridge University. Kids could be hell in the chair but were easy subjects for autosuggestion. The pain threshold could be raised, the bleeding time reduced, by getting them to watch a favourite television programme in their heads. The small patients thought it was great fun, and so did I for a while.

I was well into preventative dentistry when I met Stanley for the third time, risking the fury of the establishment by proclaiming that decay was preventable and drilling holes in teeth was a waste of patients' time and money. We passed one another in the hospital corridor, halted and looked back.

"Brid. It's Brigid Mary Rafferty," he said, smiling, holding out his hand.

"You remember my name," I said, holding out mine.

"I lost your telephone number," he said.

"I don't believe you."

"I lost it."

"The dental hospital is in the telephone book."

"I have been obscenely busy, but the exams are all done."

"Did you pass the finals?"

"Yes. I got a distinction. And you?"

"I was lucky to pass."

He was the sort of man who got distinctions in psychiatry. That night I went out to dinner with him, and a new life began. We went riding in Phoenix Park, racing in Leopardstown or the Curragh, drinking, singing and dancing until dawn in Matt Smith's bonafide pub up the Dublin mountains. It was amusing to watch the nouveau riche at play, or the rich, as at the Cattle Dealer's Ball, where I was more comfortable than Stanley. He had gone to Clongowes public school where privileged young men got the bog beaten out of them, disproving the theory that you could take the man from the bog, but not the bog from the man. Clongowes school, in exchange for a great deal of money, could and did. There was not much of the countryman left in Stanley, and I treasured the few childhood memories we shared together: picking hazelnuts in the woods, playing ball alley after mass on Sundays, eating melted-salt-filled mushrooms hot off the turf fire, and soothing nettle rash with dock leaves stuck on with spit. I thought then that the west of the Shannon childhood was the most important bond between us.

He waited weeks before he tried to kiss me and months before he tried to get me into bed. I had begun to wonder if my breath smelled. When he did kiss me he put his tongue in my mouth, the dreaded French kiss, a sign of evil intent and a mortal sin. Robin the Harrogate Protestant had been better behaved than Stanley, who tried well-known, and less well-known, tricks to get his way. Pride and the confessional prevented me from joining the despised ranks of the girls who did. So in the end he said we should marry and produced a solitaire diamond ring in Robert's Cafe in Grafton Street, where the three genteel Rhea sisters, known by the lawless clientele as Gonorrhoea, Diarrhoea, and Pyorrhoea, played extracts from Gilbert and Sullivan's operettas, behind potted palms. It seemed the final culmination of things to get married, but my stomach registered unease as he put on the ring. He had not pleaded for my hand, but had told me what we would do, and I didn't know whether this was indicative of something or not. My stomach knew something I did not.

Mary Rafferty if alive would have been gratified to see her daughter in regal ivory dress, her hair piled up around a tiara, about to be married by the Bishop of Galway. I had often wondered what I would feel on my wedding day, but as I went up the aisle on John's arm to where Stanley stood with the bishop, I felt nothing at all. Six hours after the reception we arrived at the hotel beside Lake Maria Worth in southern Austria. Everything was fine and as it should be really, so why was I crying as Stanley slept soundly, while the cicadas chorused raggedly in the burnt grass around the lake in the first light of morning? It was as if my innermost self, braced like a young cadet to attention, was shocked and shivering to be passed by. As if an awaited warm wind had swept by like an icy mistral. I put such thinking down to a tired imagination and went to sleep.

The morning brought sunshine on the lake, the sound of bells from the chapel on the hill, where the smiling young priest was not to be found at night. In the pine forest young pigs squealed, and children laughed and screamed. From our private balcony we watched swans swim on the lake, while lightning flashed and petals,

Marie McGann

ripped off the trees, whirled into the sky. A summer storm. I looked at Stanley leaning over the balcony, springy black hair silvering at the temples now, and thought that everything would be fine. We would have a fine marriage and at least four children. But somehow it was not fine, and we only had one son. Still, we had a good time on our honeymoon, dancing and drinking, swimming and drinking. Stanley got very tanned, and I got honeymoon cystitis.

Chapter Three

THE LONE WOMAN

It was a blow to my self-esteem that I, who considered myself to be finely perceptive, strongly intuitive, had not noticed something amiss with Stanley. We had had our ups and downs, but I did not think the marriage was so awful as to drive him away. Neither of us had ever brought up the subject of getting outside help, of counselling. If there had been another woman, I would have known, but then again maybe I would not. There had been no alteration in his routine, and he was always where he said he was. Or did I just assume he was at the clinic when he was not? I became unsure, uncertain of myself, and tried to look at the positive aspects of the situation. For one thing I now owned the roof over my head and had enough money in the bank to avoid having to go back to work. I didn't want to put terrified children into a hypnotic trance in the dental

chair in order to remove rampant dental decay which
they should not have had in the first place. Besides, half
of them did not speak English these days, what with the
Bangladeshis and the Hong Kong Chinese streaming in
from the old Commonwealth. I was free to do what I
liked when I felt like it, living on junk food with no dis-
approving looks to take the fun out of it and nobody
counting my drinks or checking the level of alcohol in
the bottles. There was no need to make shopping lists
in my head during the conjugal act or to lie awake on
Saturday nights listening to Stanley snoring. On the
debit side, I suffered from overwhelming mood swings.
The dawn chorus of starlings could bring with it a vio-
lent surge of rage coming up from my toes to my stomach. The bastard had planned his exit, been planning it
for God knew how long. Living a lie with his wife was
bad, but living a lie with his son was criminal, and he
should hang for it. The rage was, strangely enough, a
relief after the hurt pride, the humiliation. And what
about the neighbours? I went past the curtained windows of Mr Pocock's house to Tom and Lydia's, hoping
they would be as shocked and furious as I was. They
were sitting at the kitchen table reading newspapers
when I went in.

"Where is Disraeli?" I asked.

"Hello, darling," they both said together. "He's in the
bath."

"Stanley's gone."

They just stared at me. Tom got up, pulled out a chair
for me.

"Whiskey or rum?"

Lydia went to a kitchen cabinet.

"Whiskey."

"You mean he's left home, left you and Malachy?" Tom asked, pouring drinks for the three of us.

"Did you have a fight?" asked Lydia.

"No fight."

"Where is he gone to?" asked Tom. "Where did he say he was going to?"

"He's disappeared. He just didn't come home from the clinic.

"He'll turn up," said Lydia.

"When did this happen?" asked Tom.

"Last week. He won't turn up, Lydia. He's paid off the mortgage and put thousands in the bank."

"Are you saying he left no note, that you have no idea of his whereabouts?" asked Tom.

"I am."

"Have you rung the police?" he asked.

"I rang them. There's nothing."

"Let's hope for some good news," Tom said.

"Maybe he is gone off his head," said Lydia, and they both put their arms around me.

"Will minding Disraeli be too much for you?" asked Tom.

"He'll be company for Malachy. When are you off?"

"Tomorrow evening," said Lydia.

"We'll call you and Disraeli every day. Let's hope there will be some news," said Tom as they put their arms around me.

But there wasn't. What was I going to say if others asked? Had he not given a thought to that, him and his regard for respectability. It was lucky for me that I had Lydia and Tom Barrington-Jones in the next house but one. They had always been there for me and I for them.

I avoided the local shops, people I knew on the streets. I cultivated the anonymity of the supermarkets where I could buy liquor without being noticed. I had become aware of a change in the attitude of the man in the local off-licence, a sort of creeping ghastly familiarity in his demeanour. I clenched a metaphorical fist and waited for the appropriate time to deal with that, for no man was going to take advantage of me again. I discovered that the world had a certain attitude to the lone woman, and if I had to go out, I went to do battle. Dare anyone look at me twice. Did I not miss him? Was I lonely? Well, murderous rage was a great help in those early days, for I was too engrossed in feeling betrayed, in longing for revenge, to suffer from loneliness. Life had to go on, and I found activity like painting the window boxes a help. There was nothing to be gained in waiting for him to come home and arrange for things to be done. Mist saturated the morning air as I brushed on the yellow paint, so cheerful in the shop and now looking like infantile diarrhoea, on the wood. I didn't notice Zofia Mirska crossing the green until she called to me.

"Do be careful, Mrs Brid."

"Zofia, I should have asked you about the colour."

"It's original."

"It's shitty."

"Mix it with white."

"Come and have coffee."

I descended rung by rung without looking down. I had forgotten that I had no head for heights. We went through the hall into the kitchen at the back of the house. Zofia, a sturdy, full-breasted woman, stood a head shorter than me in high-heeled shoes. She always said she wished she had my long legs. Soft moist air drifted through an open window from the spring confusion in the garden still semi-shrouded in mist.

"I am jealous of your outlook, Mrs Brid. Mine is a brick wall."

"If I could cook like you I'd stand the brick wall, and stop calling me Mrs."

"I'll try. Our language is formal and polite."

"Something strong in your coffee?"

"It's Good Friday, but I won't say no. Who have we here?"

A small black boy regarded her from a high stool.

"I am Disraeli Barrington-Jones with a hyphen. Jesus died on Good Friday."

"How do you do?"

"I do very well."

They shook hands.

"Disraeli is our guest."

"My grandmother has influenza."

"I'm sorry to hear that."

"Do not be sorry. She is very old. Maybe she will die today like Jesus did and go to Paradise."

Disraeli smiled like a sunburst, climbed off the stool and left the kitchen.

"How old is that child?"

"Nearly nine."

"The children of today are beyond my understanding. My Anja left home for the second time last night."

"It's fashionable these days."

Loud jazz music startled us. I excused myself and ran up the stairs. Disraeli sat cross-legged on the landing, his fingers stuck in his ears.

"Malachy has that vulgar music on," he shouted.

I ran into the offending room, picked my way across the littered floor.

"Noise down," I shouted at my offspring.

"Take it easy, Mimmo," he said and obeyed.

"You'll have Mr Pocock to deal with."

"Screw him."

"Your language is terrible, Malachy."

"So is yours, Mom."

We smiled at one another. I was having to look up at him already. Something about the turn of the red head flurried my heart, stirring a childhood memory of my dead brother, long buried with violence. I turned away quickly and ran down to the kitchen where Disraeli was filling Zofia's glass without spilling any.

"What is this about Anja?"

"She is sixteen, and the police can't make her come home," said the boy.

"Bogdan and I were shocked by her friends at her birthday party. Unwashed and safety pins holding their clothes. Where are the mothers?"

"Down the boozer," said Malachy, joining us.

"The black young people never cut or comb the hair."

"It's against their religion. They is Rastafarians and they never fight."

"They get stoned on cannabis," said Malachy.

"Not all the time," said Disraeli.

"England once was fair and now it's dark," Malachy said, scratching Disraeli's curls.

"Bogdan put them out, and she took her clothes and left. She did it before her examinations, but I was ashamed to tell you."

"Ashamed to tell me?"

There was an awkward silence. Nobody spoke about Stanley's disappearance in front of the children.

"My husband stopped her going to a disco."

"Discos is bad for your ears," said Disraeli.

Zofia got up to go, her strong-boned face flushed and crumbled, and I walked with her.

"She'll come back."

"How can you be sure, you of all people? There is no news?"

"I don't really expect any."

"It's better not to expect maybe."

The avenue was ablaze with cherry and almond blossoms, the gardens springing seasonal blooms.

"What tidy gardens the English people have," said Zofia.

"Tidy gardens, tidy lives," I said wistfully.

"Strange how they don't talk or visit each other much."

"London is overcrowded, and they are reserved."

"The people talk in Cairo and Warsaw."

"Let me walk you across the green."

"I walked from Cracow to Budapest, my dear. Anja would not do this in our country, but we cannot go back."

What a depressed couple of aliens we were today. Zofia's earthy humour and my sense of the absurd usually kept us afloat.

"You think Anja will come back?"asked Zofia.

"She came back once. She'll come back when she finds out the cost of soap."

"Do you think Dr Stanley will come back?"

"He knows the cost of soap . . ."

We embraced and parted. How did I know whether it was different with him or not? A dash for freedom was a dash for freedom.

I walked back to the house remembering the difficulty we had all those years ago in explaining the location to our friends in Belgravia, who arrived cross and late at the house they could see from the hills and could not get at. It was agreeably situated in a sort of backwater, with no cinema or anything you could call a hotel. I had liked to think the suburb retained the character of a country village so beloved by the clergy and the tired city merchants long ago, though the villas, the rich meadows and the cut-throat lanes were no more. I had fallen in love with the old stone fireplace, the long sashed windows and the hawthorn bush with it's five-leaved flowers in white profusion in the tangled garden. Stanley had said its Latin name was *Crataegus oxyacantha*, but it was called heart valerian in the medical world. It calmed the heart and was valuable for the proper functioning of blood vessels and blood pressure. He had impressed me from the beginning as a man with a fund of knowledge about all sorts of things, obscure and not so obscure. I decided that if I must live in an alien land I would live there, and luckily he had agreed. The house and garden soon became my home, but the suburb took years.

Chapter Four

THE ALIEN

It began to rain after Zofia left. The half-painted window boxes, thankfully looking less faecal from the ground, would have to wait. The phone rang. To my surprise it was Hilda Uphill from across the road, wanting to call that afternoon to ask for a favour, and I heard myself inviting the woman to afternoon tea, regretting it as I did. Hilda had not bothered to see if I was managing since Stanley went, almost a year ago. I must begin to practise the word "inconvenient" which didn't trip lightly off my Irish tongue. Where there was no love, saints said, put love and you will find love. All I could afford to put between Hilda Uphill and myself was a sort of tired tolerance.

You might have expected me to engulf my anger and go into depression, but I knew better than that. I had been in clinical depression once, had been helpless in the pinions of the slow flapping vulture, and was resolved that nothing or nobody would put me back there again. Nothing ever did. I turned on the *Brandenburg* Concerto to ease the resentment in my soul. How irritable and lacking in kindness I had become of late. I would be remembered as a woman of uncertain temper if I were not careful. The boys were the only people I could stand at close range. I combed a side parting in my hair to soften the incipient hardness of my face and, seeing more grey hairs, thought I might go iron grey like the middle-class, ultra-natural Friends of the Earth in Highgate Hill. People would wonder about the suffering I endured, as they had wondered about my depression in the past. Had I not a handsome husband, a remarkably cheerful man when you came to think of his work with the deranged, a lovely son, and domestic help to enable me to come and go as I pleased? Only I didn't want to go or come anywhere. They said I was spoiled and what about the starving children in Africa? They said it could be biochemical, but the pills didn't work and I flushed them down the lavatory. Depression was a useful word for withdrawing in blocked and locked rage. Better than telling people I had no feeling for them at all. I was lifeless as a felled tree in a rain forest. And Stanley the expert, thinking I was run down, taking me to expensive restaurants, where I got down enough drink to pretend when I got home. How could I explain to that good man that I had no feeling for him at all? I had drunk to kill the despair until I read that oxygen was an effective antidepressant and took up running instead for a while.

There was no sound in the landing, and I dashed to the bathroom to shave my legs which I should never have started to do, for hairy legs did not run in my family. Always a people pleaser, I had spent my cider money on a razor under pressure from an American student who made me feel unhygienic and hirsute. Stanley had been furious the time I had gashed my shinbone and the elastoplast under my cocktail dress at the medical convention was visible to all and sundry.

In bloody-mindedness, I put on the pillar box red track suit—which Hilda Uphill thought was too much with my hair and her husband Albert thought was as jolly as a spring morning—and ran out of the house into the wood. I ran beside the softly lapping lake, where a haze of gnats hung over the water until the swallows swooped and skimmed them off before the rain came. Whooper swans and mallard ducks swam in leisurely circles, and two great crested grebes rose out of the water, wagging black-hatted heads at each other in courtship, an example of comedy and courtesy to the human race. Running had worked, though it had taken months before the shadow on my heart lifted and I stopped feeling alienated from the world I had seemed destined to view through dirty windows.

One evening I had witnessed the young sickle moon wink at the sinking sun, night greeting day, and depression had fallen away like sawn-off chains. I knew that my bones would mingle with the earth, my spirit with the stars, and I felt part of the universe. I had been able to see, for the first time in my adopted land, all the wild flowers of my childhood. They were all there this spring morning—the crocuses, the bluebells, the shepherd's purse, the scattering of tiny wood violets in the ground vegetation of bracken—and I was grateful to be alive and well, despite the past battering of my self-esteem. I vowed to run daily and force myself to pray for Stanley instead of wishing him dead. Maybe the man had gone off his head like his patients. Surely a psychiatrist in his right mind would have known better than to go off like that without a word to his son. Running had a powerful effect on my thinking.

What could Hilda want? I had not forgotten the swimming baths years ago when, one leg in my swimsuit, I had overheard Hilda say how stimulating it was for Albert and her to have the Irish practically living on the doorstep. I had gone home in tears. I had wanted to leave England at once, but Stanley said I was too sensitive, that it was meant to be a compliment, and he was not about to leave his patients. Stanley had met Hilda and Albert in the Dog & Duck, and they were faithful attenders at his parties, given to maintain the gaiety left behind in Ireland, but not once in all the years did they return an invitation. As a newcomer to the vagaries of the London social scene, I with my paper-thin skin took offence. Wanting to happily adopt the alien land, I had defended it to a notorious freeloader in a Dublin pub who said the Brits would not give you the steam off their pee. He said it to the empty bar space around him, vacated by Irishmen who were not going to give it to him either. I had told him he was a pot calling the kettle black and left before there was trouble. Later, I understood that the indigenous Londoners did not do it because they didn't need to do it. There was no tradition of hospitality in the culture of my adopted land. Fear was also a factor: they didn't do it because they were afraid to do it. They could be letting in a serial killer, or a disrupter of their lives expecting friendship.

My lungs protested with a worrying wheeze as I ran, and I determined that cigarettes and drink would have to go one day soon. With time I had conceded that the Uphills' inhospitality was not due to miserliness. Albert was a popular manager of the lucrative local funeral parlour, a great comfort to the bereaved. "Just passing over to the other side, just changing addresses" was his motto, which was stretching things a bit far for a paid up member of the Communist Party, but he was a kind man and left his atheism outside the door when at work or visiting his mum in Upper Hackney, which he did daily. He believed in enjoying this life and was partial to wearing his pale hair raffishly lengthy and flamboyant pink shirts and blue jeans as a change from funereal striped trousers and top hat. Hilda, a tall energetic woman, made the best of a curvy figure and good legs and wore her bleached blonde hair in a ponytail for getting on with the chores and up like a queen for going out to the British Legion Club in the evening. She had a habit of pursing her mouth importantly and cocking her head to one side before making a strong pronouncement, which she often did. There was not a weed to be seen in the garden in front of her house, which held regimental lines of flowers in beds as trim and round as a cardboard cut-out. Albert had crazy-paved the rest for neatness. Hilda's upwardly spiralling class aspirations were sometimes scuttled by Albert's glottal stops and dropped aitches, but she was not a woman to give up easily. I knew as I trotted out of the wood that I had begrudgingly accepted the closed doors of the community because I had no choice and now, with a twist of irony, I lived behind closed doors myself and wanted it no other way. I had found the warmth and the gaiety among the marginalised, the immigrants like myself, the gay community, where formality, frosty or not, was unknown, and now I didn't want it from ordinary English people.

I sat in the garden under the laburnum tree, pronounced by Hilda as having poisonous leaves, and waited for four o'clock. Except for the grand or the pretentious, the Irish didn't bother with afternoon tea, as tea was on the go all day. As sure as night follows day, I would not be required to spend more than two hours having afternoon tea with my guest. I watched two sly blackbirds inveigling worms out of the earth with a splay-footed slapping gait, simulating the heavy patter of rain on the grass, and an army of snails marching up the path, carrying their whorled homes on their backs. Fascinated by the flurry of activity, I forgot the expected guest until the doorbell rang. Did they wait outside, watch alert, until the hand reached the hour? I went into the hall and swung the door wide open for a smiling Hilda in pearls and a blue suit.

"Do come in."

"How nice to see an open fire."

"I like your blue suit. Do sit down."

"The dyers in Kandahar know their trade."

Hilda liked to appear knowledgeable about far-flung fashion. I, minding my manners, poured the milk in before the tea and passed the cucumber sandwiches.

"We have not been in touch, Brid, what with one thing and another, but I felt I could ask you a favour. I persuaded Arthur to let me take a Saturday job in a Polish restaurant, because the money is so good. Men know nothing about the price of clothes."

I knew they had no children, possibly because Hilda considered herself too posh to push in childbirth, so I had little sympathy for their financial problems.

"Every penny counts," I said.

"My new bridge friends have sprung a tournament on me and, while I am not ashamed of a day's work, I have not told them about it. Could you please cover for me tomorrow? If I don't go and don't cover, I'll be sacked. That is the contract."

"Sorry. I have children to mind."

"Surely your son can be left for a few hours. Just this once, please?"

Of course she was ashamed to tell her new bridge playing friends. She was nervous, hands shaking, the tiny broken veins prominent on her cheeks, and she had forgotten Malachy's name.

"I've have nobody else to ask, or I'd not have bothered you."

Suddenly it seemed easier to say I would do it but had no experience. Hilda was effusively grateful. I would be shown what to do. It was just helping out in the kitchen. At three minutes to six she drew on her dove-grey gloves and we said goodbye at the door, making the first real eye contact, grey to green, two women divided by the Irish Sea. Closing the door on my visitor, I leaned back against it. I would take my hat off to Hilda Uphill. She had eaten all the cucumber sandwiches and never mentioned Stanley in the two hours.

Chapter Five

THE POLE

You might have expected me to back out of a day's kitchen work foolishly promised to a neighbour with a superb disregard for my situation, but I did not. While I felt entitled to hurl an invective like "perfidious Albion" now and again, rattling the dead skeletons of the long oppression of my country, nobody was going to have the opportunity to fling "perfidious Hibernia" at me. Not that Hilda would be familiar with such a term, but you know what I mean. I would demonstrate that I was as good as my word. False pride and people-pleasing, striding to keep up with the inflated march of my mortified ego, compelled me to travel to the West End. I felt it to be an incredible effrontery on the part of my neighbour to expect a university gradu- ate like myself to spend a day as the kitchen slut, and resentment joined the march of my emotions. The restaurant, while safely tucked away from Hilda's bridge playing friends in a West End mews, could not be missed with its brilliant red and white paintwork, a striped canvas awning, the tables and chairs on the pavement, the music drifting out. It was a stab at street life. It was said that the face of London had changed for the worse, but surely it would be a healthy change if the people were inveigled out on to the streets to talk with each other.

A small bald man in a white apron led me to the owner's office. Mr Barowski was a shock, not at all fat, fair and fatherly as I had expected. A big silver-haired, bearded man in a lavender shirt, pale faced with dark circles under sloe-black, long-distance eyes, he looked as if he needed a good night's sleep. I had heard the Russian saying that no drawing room was complete without a Pole to grace it, so I was not too surprised by Mr Barowski's captivating manners. He prised himself out of his chair, came around the desk, bowed and kissed my hand. My heart shifted at the smile and, in spite of myself, I was swept by the charisma. In a matter of minutes I became the Lady from the Emerald Isle, a welcome replacement for Mrs Uphill and a sight for sore eyes. He would not enquire what Mrs Uphill was up to, for he knew by now that the national reserve was only skin deep. This was delivered with such an engaging grin that it did not come across as seriously racist, but I was embarrassed for Hilda who, as far as I knew, was holding nothing more exciting than a pack of cards. Mr Barowski introduced me to Roman Kowalski, the little man who was such a genius in the kitchen that taking out insurance against his kidnapping might be a good idea. His saffron *baba* incensed his rivals, not to mention his spit-roasted kid. I was to be in his safe keeping for the day.

Hilda Uphill had not prepared me for the heat of the kitchen or the smells of fish and sauerkraut. Three noisy, sweaty, head-banded youths skinned herrings and took turns stirring a cauldron of pork and sauerkraut called *bigos*, and a piglet turned on a spit over a charcoal fire. Rows of herb jars covered one wall, and Roman's saffron *baba* looked so exquisite covered in caster sugar that I believed Barowski's boast. Past dissection studies in zoology had not equipped me to remove ink sacs from squids, but stuffed squid was on the dinner menu. Roman taught me how to bind matso meal, pimentos and parmesan cheese with egg yolk, and my efforts to get the stuffing to stay in the squids afforded the trainee chefs uproarious amusement. The stuffing came squelching out as soon as I spooned it in. I lost patience and wanted to fling the tray of squids at the wall, only that would be the end of Mr Barowski as far as I was concerned, which in itself might not be a bad thing. Was it not a bit premature to look at another man when, as the saying goes, the bed was still warm after my vanished husband? Roman rescued me from such thoughts with brandy laced coffee and toothpicks to keep in the stuffing.

"We will make a cook of you if you wish, Mrs Fineekin."

"I am only here for the day, Roman."

The little man was constantly active, interrupted only by a swig of navy rum from his hip pocket when the pressure got to him. If Hilda had been honest with me about what to expect, I would certainly have brought my own. This little man was a creative genius as a teacher and exponent of his art. He taught me to paint hard-boiled eggs for Easter in scarlet, blue and gold in a simple way. The eggs were gifts for the customers and their families for the Easter festival. I had forgotten the next day was Easter Sunday; it could easily have passed me by. I felt outside, looking in, on this rich culture. I had chosen to alienate myself from the shadowy horror, the hush of Good Friday, the expectancy before the resurrection, and without the Easter faith of my childhood, I had also forfeited the joy. I remembered the bonnets, the eggs, the bells and the smells, and my father explaining that the sunlight dancing on the walls showed that God was laughing in heaven. Oh yes, I had believed him with the pure trust of childhood. Mendacity had never entered my father's heart.

Lunch with Mr Barowski somewhat dispelled my feeling of alienation. The circles beneath his eyes were less pronounced, and strong black eyebrows balanced a bony nose and experienced black eyes. He had the fine hair of his compatriots, which would have fallen out by now if it had not been so thick. A man of contradictions. Of a still, arresting awareness and a dissolute air. No wry self-deprecatory look in that face. Women were, I knew, fascinated by such a man, wondering what he got up to. Whatever it was, he must be good at it, for he certainly looked as if he did it a lot. I hoped he was not a mind reader as well and embarrassedly felt myself blush at the thought. Customers arrived and, turning on slow Slavonic music, Barowski called to Roman to demonstrate the mazurka with him. "Hoba," Roman called and leaped on to the small dance floor. Eyes closed, heads to the left, one arm about the shoulder of the other, they began to dance as deliberately and delicately as foxes on thin ice. The dance was hauntingly graceful, a tribute to vanished times and a high-headed display of grand defiance. I marvelled at the lightness of step in such a heavy bear of a man like Barowski. The customers, well-dressed middle Europeans, stood around the dance floor in rapt attention. A burly white-suited man smiled, adjusted his monocle and gestured to me from the bar.

"You will pardon me, Madame, but you should know perhaps that the button on your blouse is undone."

I looked down in embarrassment and put it right. Stanley's departure had left me mistress of my domain, but I felt threatened, unsure of my ground outside my own territory. For a moment I thought of walking out, even pushed my chair back, but something at the back of my mind restrained me. Amid a storm of applause, the men finished the dance and returned bright-eyed.

"My friend," said Barowski to the monocled man, stabbing his shirt with a forefinger, "behave or you will find yourself on the street. Nobody introduced you to the lady. The wise man does in the beginning what the fool does in the end."

The customer was not always right in this emporium it seemed. I felt flattered that Barowski had noted the incident in spite of his absorption in the dance. Eyes in the back of his head, the hallmark of the seasoned womaniser or the successful businessman, I could not tell which. He was successful enough to take an aristocratic looking customer to task for familiarity, for the restaurant was a going concern with solid cutlery, heavy linen and murals of aeroplanes, pilots, fire and smoke covering the walls.

"Miss Finucane, my customer will not cause you to blush again."

"He meant no harm. My button was undone."

"He should mind his business."

He sat opposite to me, smiling directly into my eyes so that I had to will myself not to look away, and poured bison brandy for the three of us.

"It will take the head off your shoulders, so be careful Mrs Fineekan," said Roman.

"The lady is safe with me."

They raised their glasses and waited for me to drink.

"Dodna," said Barowski, "down in one go."

I did as he said, gasping as the fiery liquid took my breath away. Barowski drew my notice to the bison on the label.

"We saved the bison in the only primeval forest left in Europe, from the Germans, the Russians, Miss Finucane. Goering's plan to steal them failed. Let us drink to that."

Problems and pains left me. The fraught morning had given me an unaccustomed appetite, and pork cutlets with cucumber in sour cream and the bison brandy gave me the energy to face the afternoon's work, which was quickly over. Mr Barowski wanted me to stay, wanted to fetch the boys, but I was tired and he accepted that. He lived in the north of London, and I was grateful to accept his offer to drive me home.

Going out into the wet London night, it was as if the moon had thrown slivers of silver into the rivulets of water running off the streets and into the gutters. Dripping tree boughs hung darkly suspended against the city skyline, and yellow street lights flared through the young spring leaves. It was as if the world was an apple found too long wrapped in paper in a loft, taken down and polished. It shone. I inebriatedly wished that happiness was an apple to be cut in half and shared with someone. Then we would need each other to make a whole. Barowski took off his jacket and covered my head from the drizzle of an April shower.

"You must be tired, Miss Finucane, after such work."

"I have seldom felt so good in my life."

I began to realise that the sooner I got home the better.

"You should not get wet now."

"It doesn't matter."

And it did not matter, anaesthetised as I was. He settled me into a Daimler parked around the corner and revving the engine set out for the north.

"Will you come with me to mass tomorrow evening?"

It seemed perfectly natural to say I would. Next morning, of course, I blamed it all on the bison brandy.

Chapter Six

THE MASS

I awoke to a loud carillon of church bells with a fearsome hangover and an assignation to go to Easter Sunday evening mass with a Polish Battle of Britain war hero. I could back out of it though, send Malachy down to say I was sick, which was true. I got out of bed and padded across the floor to the window. Haze hung like muslin over the morning sky and stretched over the distant hills. Behind me the house was strangely silent. Except for a lone linnet's warbling call, even the birds were silent. The haze began to lift, drifting away over the grey slate roof tops. Whatever might be said about Stanley's presence, his absence was palpable, and I might as well keep my appointment and get out of the house. I went to the bathroom to wash. I sat in my dressing gown at the dressing table and painted my face, trying to repair the ravages of yesterday. My eyes were like those of a dog lost on a motorway. I went downstairs wondering how long it took to adjust to sleeping alone. Embarking on a marriage was like journeying on a fast lane without lights or brakes, and mothers should be forced to counsel their daughters, but whatever my mother Mary Rafferty had been able to tell me before Shane died, there had been little in the way of conversation afterwards.

The kitchen was at its worst, and Fred had left his card under the table. At least dog dung smelt better than cat dung. I swallowed aspirin and took black coffee, and spent the day cleaning the house. At four o'clock I went upstairs and wondered what to wear.

"Wear the dress with no back," said Malachy, lying across my bed.

Disraeli sat contentedly painting his thumbnails red at the dressing table.

"Not to church, Malachy."

"Poles like their women flash."

"Manners, Malachy. I'm not a Polish woman."

"They marry their own kind in the end."

"I am only going to church, for God's sake."

I chose a lime green suit.

"Poles are bad for women," said Disraeli, painting with care around his cuticle. "They make women have babies and then they won't answer the phone."

From where was that child getting such information? Lydia and Tom would kill me when they came home. I worriedly struggled into stockings, looked over at Malachy looking so defenseless, so lacking in Disraeli's supreme confidence, that my heart shrank.

"Don't worry about me, darlings. I won't be long."

I put my nose to the back of Malachy's neck and laid my face to Disraeli's curls.

"Stay as long as you like, Mimmo. I'll mind Disraeli."

"I will mind myself," said Disraeli.

When the doorbell rang I was glad of the silver fox jacket Stanley had given me. Mr Barowski was resplendent in a light grey suit, scarlet tie, silver hair brushed back off his forehead, beard neatly clipped.

"You are a sight for sore eyes, Miss Finucane."

He bowed and kissed my hand and, as I got into the car, I waved at the young faces peering from the upstairs window. Loneliness gripped me to be leaving them, crazily going to mass with a stranger. I blamed Hilda Uphill, I blamed the bison brandy, and lastly I blamed myself for not counting the drinks. As we got out at the church I saw at once that I should have worn a hat. A fur hat. I had forgotten women were expected to cover their heads. Except for my wedding day and Malachy's christening, I had not entered a church since Shane's funeral. The stone church was small, forbidding, and my apprehension grew as we climbed the steps. The stone carving of the Last Judgment over the doric portico was a chastisement, a face slap, but the interior, aglow with light filtering in through wonderful coral and russet stained-glass windows, eased my discomfort. Barowski led me up the aisle to a front seat, excused himself with an insultingly abstracted expression and virtually left me at the altar. To sing in the choir, he said. Dismayed and resentful, I genuflected awkwardly and knelt beside an astrakhan-hatted woman, the wood hard beneath my knees. Carnations red and white, the Polish colours, banked the high altar, tall wax candles flickered on zodi-acally painted walls, and a crouching white eagle, the symbol of Poland, surmounted the statue of the Black Madonna of Poland. Helmetted German soldiers were painted standing over dying Polish soldiers in the window to my left, and the magnificent gold filagreed candelabra hanging over the altar would fetch enough money to feed the starving in Central Africa for years.

A low decibelled vocal sound backed by the organ rang out as a procession of priests flanked by candle-bearing altar boys filed out of the sanctuary and up the altar steps. The congregation arose as strong voices swelled in haunting minor key harmony. Sudden tears scalded the back of my nose, my eyes, and my throat constricted painfully. It had been years since I had cried without a handkerchief at mass and wiped my nose on my holy communion veil. I struggled to my feet, furtively scrabbled in my bag for tissues, found a shred and blew my nose on it. Mary Rafferty had said you could tell a woman's breeding by her handbag, shoes and handkerchief. Tough. Tears and snot in a convent school was one thing though, but unacceptable in a red-haired grown woman in this congregation, without enough respect to cover her head. I bet they thought I was a Jewess. Serve Barowski right if I disgraced him, abandoning me without prior warning among strangers in this strange place.

I distinguished a deep rich voice as his in the "Kyrie Elision". It rang around the walls, echoed to the rafters in the nave and stunned the angry dialogue in my head. I found myself wondering if the room would spin around when he kissed me, for I was already assuming he would. An unaccustomed passion assailed me suddenly, causing my knees to tremble and my stomach to knot painfully. I sat down among the standing congregation until the "Kyrie" was over, Barowski's voice still, and the pain subsided, leaving me spent.

The head and shoulders of Christ Pantocrator in gold mosaic filled the apse ceiling; black Middle Eastern eyes, pools of sadness over the fall of Jerusalem, over Poland, hands raised in triumph of love over hatred. Our Lady's life in fresco on a stuccoed wall filled me with self-pity. Poor Mary, bowing to God's will; poor women bowing to men's will, suffering in childbirth. Even God was a male, glaring at but not stopping the Germans while angels held the dying Poles. John Rafferty had said that the state of the world was not God's fault, that man had free will. What good was free will to me? Headstrong as a donkey, Mary Rafferty had said. Like Christ. I challenged the black eyes in the ceiling. No wonder they had put Him away, turning everything upside down like that. One marriage, one life, He had said. He was spot on. Once was enough. Had our marriage been awful enough to drive Stanley away? Neither of us had invited Christ into our marriage as we had been reared to do, but then did He need a special invitation, for God's sake. When I ran out of people to blame, I blamed God.

I had early become suspicious of a God who let his Son suffer like that. John Rafferty said that God's plan was like looking at tapestry from the back; you couldn't see the whole picture. All the same, I was not convinced. Later, of course, I had less time for a God who didn't save Shane. I knelt with the congregation, glad that I had escaped the great Aunt Sally, the Catholic Church, people liked to hurl things at, the interminable rosaries, the fear-riddled confessions. I was not going to be sucked back into the stupendous claims of Christianity, the slow slog of the spiritual life. An altar boy swung a burner and there was the long forgotten smell of incense. "Do this in memory of Me." I felt a lowering sensation of guilt for turning down the ancient invitation, slighting the offer of friendship, not bothering to get ready before I came. I had come either to get out of a house still filled with Stanley's absence after all this time, or to see the Pole again or maybe both. Barowski had not given me enough warning about attending a mass. I tried to shift blame to Barowski, but it would not stick.

I could not make him out. He was too successful to be careless, too confident to need to show a strange woman off, and there were less risky ways of seducing a woman. A church was the last place for that kind of thing, but it was original, I'd give him credit for that. Perhaps he was his own man like my quiet father, who had died believing in God's plan despite years of marriage to my mother, a fiery member of the women's branch of the IRA, the Cumann na mBan. My father John Rafferty had an unusual brain. The analytical, logical left side was balanced by the creative, imaginative right side. A Shakespearean scholar, he was as much at home in the literary world as he was in that of physics and mathematics.

"I will bind up the wounds of the broken-hearted," sang the priests from the high altar. Forlornly I sat up, wiping tears and blowing my nose with soggy tissue

shreds. *"Panis angelicus, fiat panis hominum . . ."*
Barowski's voice in the ancient Easter hymn filled the
spaces of my mind. The atmosphere filled with joy, and
a current of high-voltage energy flowed through my
body, loosening my throat, clearing my sinuses, watering
the backs of my eyeballs, tingling through my limbs to
fingers and toes. My skin burned. Was I to become a
human steak in a holy microwave, destined to end in a
heap of ashes? Barowski would have to sweep me up in
a dustpan. I hoped if it came to that he would be thor-
ough and not leave charred remains under the seat. Then
it seemed to me that I received a benediction that was
quite unlike the blessings in the doom and gloom of the
confessional, and all the dross of my past life was
absolved. All the lucid cruelties inflicted on those around
me. The abysmal selfishnesses, the false misrepresenta-
tions, the sham and counterfeit of my life, and worst of
all, my cowardly opting for coldness of heart. All the
little foxes that destroy the vineyard. I was possessed by
a fierce detachment as the congregation rose and began
to file out of the church, so that when Barowski
approached, I looked on him as from afar and watched
his smile tighten, the light shift in his dark eyes.

"You enjoyed our ceremony, Miss Finucane?"

"Mrs Finucane. You did not tell me you sang."

"You liked our music?"

"I was amazed."

With an effort I gave him my hand and rose to join
him. It was not until we drove away that I asked him
why he brought me, a stranger, to a Polish mass and on
such a special day.

"It was because I thought you should not be lonely any more."

"I am not lonely, Mr Barowski."

"The eyes do not lie, Miss Finucane."

I said nothing, drew back, for whether he was friend or foe, an intruder is an intruder.

"That is not the way home, Mr Barowski."

"All roads lead to home, Miss Finucane."

"The children are on their own."

"You'll be home shortly."

Where was he taking me? Thoughts of rape crossed my mind, but he was too big to attempt it in the car. I knew nothing of him, and while he didn't seem the type, singing like an angel, you never knew these days.

"In order to make London one's home, it is necessary to stop before sights like the skyline of London from Highgate Hill."

So I, who chose to cling to the idea that the Sceptred Isle had little to recommend it, saw for the first time the domes and spires of the city, St Paul's Cathedral, the russet roof tops below stretching to the far-off hills. He lit two cigarettes and gave me one. I relaxed.

"There are nights I wish to hear seagulls screeching along the banks of the Wistula, the wash of the river at high tide, the cry of the storks on the chimney tops."

In the close confines of the car, the man's sadness moved me, fears evaporated and when he took my hand, I did not mind. I was familiar with murderous homesickness, the loss of the sounds of one's country. I felt it now like a blow to my well-defended heart, as if I had never managed to get over it, and we sat without speaking, an invisible bond growing between us. Aliens in captivity. It was as if we had made love already, had penetrated one another and come to rest. He opened a window and the smell of the earth, of the woods, came in in small gusts of air. He replaced my hand and, turning the key in the ignition, started the engine.

"Red eyes are not for children, Miss Finucane."

"Stop calling me Miss. I have a son."

"I know that. I call you Miss because your husband is gone."

"How do you know that?"

"It does not signify."

Hilda Uphill had spread the news. He parked outside the house and got out to open the door. Stanley had never done that after I married him.

"I had wondered who lives here."

"Now you know."

"Now I know. You are in the telephone book?"

"Yes. Have you far to drive home?"

"A matter of minutes."

He waited until I turned the key and opened the front door before he got back into the car. Some rapist. He had not even attempted to kiss me.

Chapter Seven

BANK HOLIDAY

In the cities and towns of this part of the world, the Easter Monday bank holiday can bring a stillness without and a stillness within for those of us at peace with our gods and ourselves, but sadly not for the likes of me. I got up the minute I awoke with the racing dialogue already beginning in my head and went into the boys' bedroom. My uncertain heart swelled at the sight of the three sleeping heads on the pillows. Fred had no way of knowing he was a dog. Malachy opened his eyes.

"Hi there, Mimmo," he whispered.

"Hi there, kiddo."

"How was the Polish cavalier?"

"He sang at mass."

"Will he come here?"

"Maybe."

"Will we like him?"

"He's a nice person."

"You better call Mrs Mirska. She wants you to go for dinner tonight."

"Did you tell her where I was yesterday?"

"No fear."

"She knows already, I'd say."

"Poles are racists."

"No more than others."

"Mr Mirski says he'd step over his dying daughter for marrying a black man. Will Disraeli hate us when he grows up?"

"Don't be silly."

"He is called after Benjamin Disraeli, an English prime minister."

"He was also the first Earl of Beaconfield and a Jewish gentleman."

"He must have been rich to buy his way in then. The Poles call Jews mountaineers in case anyone is listening."

"Oh God, Malachy, you cannot tar everyone with the same brush."

I fled from such worrying cynicism and my own unfortunate choice of words. Something would have to be done about his world view, but what or how? Father Joe would say that Malachy's contempt for the world was a projection of his own feeling of worthlessness since his father left him, and hopefully it would pass. Should I consider bereavement counselling for him, whether Stanley was still alive or not? I would think about it as I hoovered the sitting room. Exhibiting the early symptoms of paranoia, I closed the windows in case Mr Pocock next door would hear and offer to do it. Mr Pocock was something big in the city. He always kept himself to himself and we were happy to let him, so I was shocked and embarrassed when he smilingly raised his bowler hat to me on the street, saying meaningfully that if he could be of any assistance whatsoever not to hesitate to ask. The word that Stanley was long gone was spreading fast then. I had often thought that Mr Pocock would make a good husband for somebody. Somebody else. He was not among the ten percent of sexually magnetic men with a high pheromone level who could get any woman they clapped an eye on. I would not put it past Adam Barowski to be in that top ten percent. The carpet began to look less well lived in as the cleaner lifted broken biscuits and squashed jelly babies in front of the television. God knew what they had seen on television when I was out with Barowski. At least Fred was incorruptible. I dialled Zofia's number.

"You rang, Zofia?"

"Anja is coming for her sewing machine tonight."

"That's good news."

"Bogdan and I want you to come to dinner tonight. Sorry for the short notice. Do come. Pan Barowski is coming and I believe you have met."

"You're well informed."

"Every Pole in north London knows you were in Devonia Church yesterday."

"Maybe I should have thought twice."

"Don't be angry, Mrs Brid. You honoured us by going there. Pan Barowski will expect you."

"That's presumptuous of him."

"Blame me. I told him you'd come."

"I have little choice then."

"7.30 for 8pm. Thank you, my dear."

Stung, I put the phone down. He might have called me himself and not got somebody else to do the inviting. Still, it was not his house and not for him to invite.

"We don't want no babysitters," said Disraeli.

"You better get your hair done," said Malachy."

Katy Quinn, my long-term friend and hairdresser, said I should come at once, as there was no knowing what the place would be like later on. Keeping the Lord's day or bank holidays was grand for them as had time. As I walked to Katy's house, raindrops hung like solitaire diamonds from the branches of the trees lining the rain-washed pavements. Traffic was negligible, as hordes of Londoners were soaking up the sun, the gin or the *aragi* in places like Torremolinos or Marrakech. Stepping through Katy's open front door past the picture of the Sacred Heart and the loaded coatstand, my spirit lifted at the noise in the kitchen where Katy ran her business and the clients had raised her children. It had been worth changing nappies and heating bottles for the life and fun in Katy Quinn's, and beside she was the best for miles around with a certificate in trichology and a distinction in trichopathology. I was welcomed, as always, as if I had been on a dangerous expedition, and it warmed my heart. I always felt at home in spite of, or maybe because of, the crowd, the littered floor, the cigarette smoke and the constant tea making, which latter I was forbidden to do, as Katy said I should leave it to those as knew how.

"Any sign of your man?" Katy asked.

"No sign."

"Good riddance. A man is like a bus. Miss one and there's another on the way."

Katy regulated the hot water and guided my head into the sink.

"Open countenance we Irish have, in spite of our cunning. The unsettling is on your face. Well rid of him one minute, missing him the next. Glad of freedom one minute, rage at the bastard next. Hurt pride is like a cattle's murrain."

"Murrain?"

"The running shits, or diarrhoea to be grand. It's a killer. Any woman worth her salt wants to be first out the door, if there's leaving to be done."

Katy knew about hurt pride. Her husband Patrick, or Mr Quinn as she called him—whether out of respect for the head of the house or derision at his grandiose alcoholic behaviour, nobody could decipher—spent his days holding court in the Dog & Duck. A skilled man had to be careful not to go down the wrong road of life, he said. Over-qualified for all the roads, it seemed, Mr Quinn saw himself as a perspicacious man, a solver of knotty political world problems and a renderer of "I'll Take You Home Again, Kathleen" in a heartbreaking tenor voice until there wasn't a dry eye in the pub. Katy Quinn had first-hand experience of every negative emotion known to the human species.

"I've met a man," I said.

"Did you go to bed with him yet?"

"I've only met him twice."

"Either you will or you won't and you know that

already. One look at Mr Quinn and I was destroyed entirely."

She whipped a net around my hair, put foam pads on my ears and the drier over my head. Katy was right. Sexual energy existed between the Pole and myself. Whether we acted on it was another matter. As an abandoned wife I was unclear about my future. Katy lifted the lid when my hair was dry.

"They say in Connemara that you cannot mend a broken vase. You may restore it, but it is not the same. Be careful and come to see me soon."

"Maybe the glue is stronger these days."

"Wouldn't that be lovely," said Katy, hugging me goodbye. "Call me for babysitting. Mine are old enough to be left."

Black rooks wheeled around the tall belfry of the clock tower, and pigeons flew high in formation, bellies flashing silver in their twice daily flight circling the suburb. I felt lonely to be leaving the Irish house. Stanley did not mix with the working-class Irish community, or the working-class English either. He refused to drink in the British Legion Club, surely a place of great safety from free consultations. Stanley the policeman's son, slicing lemons for his gin and tonic. Sometimes I judged him to be a West Briton, a deadly insult in Dublin for the pretentious Irishman ashamed of his roots. Like the time he was furious to find me pouring tea for four Irish road workers in the kitchen. The men had known at once, become falsely obsequious, doffing their caps, and left. Stanley had turned on the bath water aggressively, and I had wept over the teacups in the sink. I had loved to hear the soft country accents, the natural courtesy of the men, hailing from a rich culture, rejected as illiterate peasants in England, driven to the pubs for warmth and music. I had banged the cups in the sink and blamed academic success for going to his head.

Walking home through the Broadway, I wondered whether I had loved Stanley. I stopped and gazed at the South American pacu fish in the window tank of the aquarium, at the shoals of tiny silver and harlequin fish swimming through the green plants. How I wished to be in a green subterranean world on the ocean bed, safe from the world I inhabited and the likes of Adam Barowski. Had I ever known Stanley, so busy had we been dancing, drinking and going to the races? And now it was too late. He would not be coming back now after all this time.

Chapter Eight

THE DINNER PARTY

I had gone to the trouble of having my hair done, and while I was not accustomed to socialising without an escort, I better get used to it or close my front door on the world like the Londoners. Mind you, I did leave it to the last minute, struggling as I was with conflicting feelings about meeting Barowski in such circumstances. A grey blanket of desolation drove me out into the garden. Starlings squabbled in the hawthorn bush, and two cats fought and screamed under Disraeli's trolley car. That did it. I chose a narrow green dress which swirled around the calves of my legs.

"Don't answer the door," I said to the boys, ensconced with Fred and ice lollies at the television.

"You can ring us to see we're OK," said Malachy.

"Your eyes is shiny," said Disraeli, holding his lolly conveniently for the dog.

They were engrossed in the programme as I left the room, and I felt there was no problem in leaving them for a while.

When I was ready down to my favourite perfume, I stood in the hall to check my purse.

"Most adults is lying pigs."

I was shocked to hear a balanced child like Disraeli make such an indictment, wavered in my track, then went out the hall door vowing to deal with that at the first opportunity. I knew that Disraeli was very angry with his parents, blaming them for not coming home to him sooner, and with Stanley. Children should be more important than a half-dead grandmother, as Malachy, his best friend in all the world, should be too important for his father to leave him like that. Worriedly I walked across the green, wishing I had asked Katy Quinn to babysit, vowing to give the boys more time, more guidance. Also, I knew what lollies did to the teeth and Fred had worms occasionally, had them all the time for all I knew, and I was letting them do whatever kept them quiet.

Zofia was up to something. Stanley and I had not socialised with the Polish couple, and I had seldom met Zofia's husband in the years I had known her at the delicatessen. I felt like an actress coming on in the second act with no knowledge of the lines or the role. John Rafferty had told me I was a child of God and as good as the rest when I had gibed at the hornpipe competition for the under-eights. I had said I could not go on the stage, and John had said I could, and who would see my silver buckled shoes, my Tara brooch, my embroidered shawl and kilt if I did not? I had gone on the stage to show off my clothes and won a silver cup for dancing instead. It had been a long time since I felt like a child of God.

The lights were on all over the Mirski's house. Anxiety and resentment tightened my stomach as I approached the house. Barowski had not bothered to call me. Serve the Poles right if they had nothing further to gossip about. I knew they thrived on gossip, strongly cloistered as they were from the host community. At the same time I caught myself hoping that the dark circles under Barowski's eyes were not due to kidney trouble as Mary Rafferty would have had it. Something could be done about a dissolute life but not chronic nephritis. As I rang the chiming bell, I braced myself to face Bogdan Mirski, a man who hit his daughter with a leather belt.

Zofia's joyful face gladdened me as she led me into a hall dominated by a picture of the Black Madonna of Czestochowa and the smell of fine cooking. I had forgotten to bring flowers, but before I could worry about it I was ushered into the sitting room, where two men stood with backs to a crackling log fire at the far end of the room. Barowski stood head and shoulders taller than the burly figure of the host, who looked older and balder than when I had last seen him. Pan Mirski came forward, bowing from the waist to kiss my hand.

"I am honoured you visit my home, Mrs Finucane."

His home, not their home, I noted sourly, smiling, saying I was happy to be there.

"I believe you have met Pan Barowski."

Barowski came forward, bowed, kissed my hand and held it for a moment.

"We waited with impatience, Miss Finucane."

He smiled and it flashed in the dark eyes. I felt a blow to the heart and kept my eyes on his amber-coloured tie before turning away. I saw the stumps of fingers as Pan Mirski handed me a glass of sherry.

"A legacy from Russia, my dear Mrs Finucane."

He had seen me looking.

"I'm sorry," I said, embarrassed to be caught.

"Be glad instead that I did not end in Lubyanka," said Pan Mirski, "or shot in the back of the head."

"With the thousands of Polish officers in Katyn Forest," said Barowski.

"When I should not have the pleasure of your charming company this evening, Madam," said Mirski, with a refined dash of flattery.

We stood around the fire, and I was glad of my highest heels, the shot silk green dress and of the sherry warming my stomach. I realised I had not eaten all day and must be careful to watch my drinking.

"Pan Mirski fought a gallant war with the Eighth Army," said Barowski.

"That was nothing in comparison to our grandfathers, chasing invading tanks on horseback," said Mirski deprecatingly.

There was a camaraderie between the two men. I was afraid to make eye contact with Barowski. I was relieved when Zofia called us into the dining room, which easily held the richly laid table, candlelight shining on silver cutlery and crystal glassware. Pan Mirski said grace in Polish and then in English for me.

I was to sit at his right hand. Barowski drew my chair out and seated himself opposite. Pan Mirski poured chilled vodka, and Zofia brought beetroot soup, then took her place at the foot of the table near the kitchen. Mirski indicated the empty set place at the table.

"It is our custom to leave a place for the uninvited guest."

"It's the same in the Irish culture. Perchance to seat a passing angel," I said.

"I propose a toast to our charming hostess."

The men waited with raised glasses until we ladies drained ours. Zofia cleared the soup plates and returned with a platter of roast pork, wild mushrooms, red cabbage and young potatoes.

"It is time to drink *bruderschaft* with Mrs Finucane," said Mirski, flinging his napkin over his arm.

Barowski brought tall crystal glasses from the sideboard, which he placed for the others and himself. Walking around the table, he curved a warm and heavy hand on the back of my neck. I didn't know whether that was the spontaneous affection of a demonstrative man or a proprietorial sexual advance, but I felt my face flush.

"We do not feel free to use Christian names without this ceremony," said Mirski.

I was invited to stand, to link arms with each person, to kiss, to shake hands, to address the others by first name. Barowski put a glass into my hand and, linking right arms, we drank together. As we kissed on both cheeks, I tried to fix my gaze on the amber tie, but the lively dark eyes caught mine as we drew apart. Stricken I turned away, forcing a smile for Zofia.

"I hear the Irish are famous for hospitality," said Adam, as I was to call him from now on.

"The Poles also," said Bogdan.

"The Poles are famous for boasting also," said Adam.

Adam wore a gold ring on the fourth finger of his right hand. The French, I knew, wore the wedding ring on that finger. Fruit compote and cream laced with sherry followed.

"Will Margaret Thatcher get in again?" I asked, desperate for something to say.

"I'm afraid so," said Adam. "Michael Foot is too much of a gentleman to fight such an unknown breed."

"Every true Pole will vote for her to keep the Marxists and the Trotskyites in check," said Bogdan.

"His wife should burn his duffle coat and make him speak up so people could hear him," said Zofia, ignoring Bogdan.

"A woman prime minister is not more phenomenal than a Polish pope," said Adam.

"I fear for the life of Karolinky Woytyla," sighed Zofia.

"You are foolish to fear for a man who has no fear," said Bogdan.

Despite her papal sentimentality, the tone of his voice was too dismissive, and I thought that my friend was probably not conscious of being diminished in this house. She had played the role, worn like an old top coat, too long.

"May I telephone the children, please?"

"Of course. Show Brid to the telephone, Zofia."

"Is all well, Malachy?"

"Yeah, man. We got chicken and chips."

"You're not allowed to use the chip pan."

"We do it in the oven. A man rang after you left."

"What man?"

"Adam something. Are you having a good time?"

"A very good time."

And suddenly I was having a very good time, inordinately glad he had taken the trouble to secure my presence. I returned to the table and the fruit compote, and saw the wedding ring on Zofia's right hand. There was no place for a ring on the stump of Bogdan's right hand. Surreptitiously I checked Adam's right hand again. He was married then. Well, so was I for that matter. All the same, a wife at home changed everything. How unintelligent of me to expect a man like that to be single. I accepted a full glass of liquor.

"To the ladies for the first time," said Bogdan.

Bogdan led me into the sitting room, while Zofia and Adam went to make coffee.

"I believe you have met Adam before?"

"Briefly."

"He was awarded the *Virtuti Militari*, the highest award for bravery in battle."

So he was a war hero then.

The ding dong bell pealed and we heard Zofia go to the front door. Uncomfortable as I was, I was further disturbed by rows of grim-faced, bulging-eyed male heads in plaster on the wall beside my chair. The married hero certainly came from a grim and pathetically sad culture, and it was as well not to get drawn into that.

"Replicas of the infamous Heads of Wawel, Brid. A cross-section of Italian dignitaries and peasants given to Poland by the unpopular Queen Bona Forsza. She decorated the ceiling of the Hall of Heralds in the castle with 195 of them. No wonder the Poles disliked her."

I put down my glass of vodka. A strapping black-hatted girl followed a knock on the door. Not at all the cowed Slavonic teenager I might have expected, but the high flat cheekbones, almond-shaped eyes and round arched, short-toothed smile bespoke the Pole in Anja Mirska.

"Our daughter Angelica. To what do we owe this visit?"

"Hi. For my sewing machine."

"If you chose to live elsewhere, nothing belongs to you here."

"Bollocks."

"Leave your gutter language outside and show some courtesy to our guest."

Anja sat, flinging a booted foot up on a knee. She wore striped dungarees and a trailing orange scarf. Bogdan went red.

"Are you a refugee?" she asked of me.

"We are all immigrants," I said.

"My parents are not. They are refugees, like the Polish government in exile. Some still run in the woods for rifle practice."

The tone was so sardonic that I could well understand where the leather belt came in. Neither Bogdan nor Zofia were equipped to deal with such insolence. Zofia came in with coffee and an anxious expression.

"My grandfather chased German tanks on horseback."

"You may joke about the quaint ways of the cavalry,

Miss, but we became troublesome resistance fighters on the ground and won a year's respite for the Western Allies," said Bogdan.

"Small thanks you got, not even invited to march in the 1946 British Victory Parade," said Anja.

"You were told often enough that there was no choice. Stalin would not have liked it," said Adam.

"Why did the Polish pilots in the British air force tear up their invitations then?"

Nobody replied, as Bogdan went around with the brandy bottle. Adam was probably one of those principled pilots, I thought. Not that it mattered now. A married man living in the past.

"Have you children?" Anja asked me.

"One son."

"Only children like me are either spoiled or deprived. We either bully our boyfriends or become promiscuous."

"And which are you?" I asked, incensed.

"Both, I expect," said the young and beautiful Angelica Mirska, whose legs, unlike her mother's, were long and slender. Longer than mine. Anja rolled a cigarette and the smell of cannabis filled the room. The parents seemed oblivious, but Adam gazed intently at Anja. I refused the brandy, feeling middle-aged and jealous, and tried to focus my thoughts elsewhere.

It was many years since an Irishman with good teeth had talked me into smoking cannabis, and while I had had no idea how I got home, I was fully clothed and alone when I woke up. He obviously had a streak of Catholic decency in him, not like Stanley. I had lied to the priest who had wanted to know whether I was on or in the bed with Stanley and had to confess the lie down the other end of the church. I had been told to stay away from the drink and the man, but I had done neither. I married the man and took up the drink instead. Suddenly I knew that I had had too much to drink and better leave while I could exit with some dignity.

I stood up, saying I must go home to the children and thanking the hosts for a lovely and interesting evening. Adam wanted to drive me home, but I said I wanted to walk across the green. What was the point in letting him, a married man, drive me home? They fussed around me, finding my coat, helping me on with it, not wanting me to go. I felt sad for them. People without a country like myself, only I had left mine voluntarily, while they were tricked out of theirs. I could repatriate, and some day I might, but not they. I managed to embrace them quickly and leave. Looking back, I could see them standing, waving, at the gate. Like aunts in country houses long ago.

Chapter Nine

THE CABLEGRAM

Telegrams are daily trivia, so commonplace are they in some people's lives, but not in mine. I associate them with trouble. Therefore the cablegram on the hall mat in the morning caused my heart to race, my legs to tremble. I picked it up, sat down on the bottom step of the stairs. It could not be from Adam Barowski, to whom I had said goodbye six hours earlier, and who was most probably not out of bed yet. Oh God, let it not be bad news, I thought, like the atheist in the front line trench, though Father Joe said there was no such thing. How could it be bad news, when there was nobody left to die in the family?

I fingered and peered at the cablegram as if I could decipher its contents through the envelope. It did not occur to me that it might be from Stanley, because I really had written him off for good. No hard-working man parts with such money as he'd put into my bank on a whim, and least of all Stanley, who was careful to the point of stinginess. I opened the green envelope with trembling hands. I read "Hoping return London summertime. If unable, please arrange to come here."

It had been sent from Wad Medani, the Sudan, on the seventeenth of March, St Patrick's Day if you please. A patriot to the last ditch. My God, wait until Tom and Lydia heard this. I felt numb. A brave morning light filtered through the red and green Victorian tulips in the window above my head. The *Guardian* reported trouble between the Muslim north and the Christian south in the Sudan and President Nimeri's intention to throw all the country's alcohol into the Nile. How was Stanley managing without his gin and tonic in a dry country? Serve him right for walking out on his responsibilities without a backward glance and letting two years and two months go by without a line.

The first thing to understand was that he was alive. He had not gone off his head and committed suicide, and there was a note of authority in the cablegram which belied a mental disorder of any kind, it seemed to me. I had lived with that air of authority, and I had resented it. I had never taken kindly to being told what to do, and anything smacking of an order was anathema to me. Delia, unlike my mother Mary Rafferty, seldom told me what to do. She led and I followed because I trusted her as well as loved her. It was the same with Shane.

"Please arrange to come here," I read again. I was being ordered to travel to an outlandish country without any explanation. He must think me a soft fool. Sending a comprehensive letter was surely no more difficult than this cryptic few words, unless he was in jail, with letters censored or forbidden. Still, if he could sneak out the cablegram, he could sneak out a letter. Did he expect me to waltz off to Africa just because he said so? If he did, then his thinking was off beam. Putting all that money into my account, he had probably intended to get out for good, so what had changed his mind? Did he think he could do that to me, walk out, then walk back just like that? I began to pull myself up by the banisters, but my back muscles contracted in agonising spasm and I was immobilised.

It was cold in the hall, but I hesitated to shout for fear of frightening the boys. What was Malachy going to think of this news? The world was full of imponderables and intolerable pain. I had no choice but to sit where I was until Malachy came down.

"Why are you sitting there like that, Mom?"

"My back's seized up, darling. I've had a cablegram from Daddy. He is alive in Africa."

I gave it to him and watched his face sharpen and lose colour as he read.

"I thought he was dead. Where's the Sudan?"

"In Africa. Near Egypt."

"Why wait to contact us until now?"

"Maybe he was in prison, or had amnesia."

"Bollocks, Mom."

"Language, Malachy. We can't judge without the facts."

"I can judge if I like. He never bothered to say good-bye."

Disraeli came down and they tried to help me to my feet, but I could not stand. Malachy had never spoken to me like that before. I had not thought him capable of it, but then had I really thought of anyone except myself and my wounded pride at being shown up as a laughing stock to the neighbours? Malachy rang for an ambulance and Zofia Mirska, and Disraeli covered me with the Donegal rug. Within a couple of hours I was in the local cottage hospital with my legs in traction. To stretch the spine, the Pakistani doctor said, as he gave me an injection to relax the muscles. It also relaxed my mind, and very soon I drifted off to sleep, knowing that Zofia would see the boys were safe.

The night matron woke me out of my sleep, shining a torch on my face to see if I were alive. My mind swam with the thought that Stanley was alive. I was neither glad nor sorry, just confused. There was nothing I could do about it in the hospital; the respite was welcome. The activity, sounds and smells of the ward triggered off memories of my short-lived youthful escapades as a trainee nurse, some hilarious, some painful. The bent heads of the night nurses under the pool of light dragged me sharply back to the first time I ever saw Stanley when we were young and full of hope. Loneliness overwhelmed me, but I knew what to do about it when I got home. I would go to the British Legion Club, where the faces would light up to see me, and I would sit drinking in the noisy smoky warmth among the friendly mums and nans watching darts or playing bingo while their Sunday joints cooked slowly and the Yorkshire batter lay ready in bowls. And Zofia had called the ward with the good news. Lydia and Tom were coming home next week. I'd have them back in my life as well as the British Legion.

Malachy was only five the day they arrived, and Stanley had returned from mowing the front lawn smelling of rum, announcing that we had new West Indian neighbours. Not a word about calypso parties and the price of property going down. Grudgingly I remembered Stanley's more sterling qualities. He had often exhibited great patience and control, like the time I had accelerated instead of braking and nearly killed a woman on the zebra crossing. Malachy had screamed at me to take my foot off the incinerator, but Stanley said not a word and managed to stop the car just in time. I always over reacted to life, and he with his inner discipline responded with cool.

Tom and Lydia were cool, too. Everybody but me. I had no inner discipline. If the Barrington-Joneses were disappointed in the welcome they got, in the superiority shown them every day in London, they never showed it. Nobody could say they were non-contributors to the society of their adoption, she with her nursing and he with his teaching. Tom could pass for white except for his hair, and Lydia had a stunning smile and body, and while they could aspire to spiral upwardly in society like Hilda Uphill, they were comfortable in their own skins and didn't bother. I loved them for that as well as for the constant solace they brought me. Funny how easily they had accepted Stanley's departure, but they stayed closer to me after that, ringing up and popping in. I yearned for them to come back.

The ward sister said I looked exhausted and should avail of the rest. No wonder, with all that travelling inside myself. I decided to discharge myself as soon as they removed the traction, flushed the anti-inflammatory pills down the toilet and took a bath supervised by a young nurse. My limbs shook, and I knew that I should stop drinking, but then I had said that for years. My stomach was concave with loss of weight and my big toenails ingrown, a legacy from the wracking leather shoes of my nursing days, as brief as they had been. It was as well my behaviour had shortened those days in the hospital before I picked up something irreversible. I had picked up a husband, of course, and while I had thought that fact was irreversible, I did not know any more. A husband wasn't like an ingrown toenail. You could cut a V shape in a toe nail, so it would grow into the gap and away from the sides, but you could not do that with a husband. Yet maybe I had cut a V shape in my marriage without knowing it, and Stanley had grown into the gap and away from me. What could he want from me now after all this time? I got a taxi home and, after a breathless welcome from the children, went straight to bed.

The boys made a great fuss, and we lived on takeaway food until I was strong enough to stand in the kitchen. Malachy cut my toenails and Disraeli painted them red, for I was not to bend down. Adam Barowski had rung and Malachy had told him I was not allowed visitors in the hospital. I said I could have had visitors and Disraeli, sitting behind me on the sofa brushing my hair, said visitors was a pain. They had blocked him and he had let them. I checked disappointment at its spawning. What could I expect of a married man, and more to the point, what could I now expect as a married woman?

Malachy and I drank hot chocolate sitting on the sofa together one night after Disraeli was asleep, watching swollen, inky black rain-filled clouds scudding across the moon, obscuring the church spire.

"Would you go there if he can't come?"

"I don't know."

"If you go I'm going."

"You mustn't miss exams."

"He didn't ask me to come."

His voice trembled, but when I laid my head on his shoulder, he patted it as if I were a child.

"I'm glad he isn't dead, Mom."

We embraced and he helped me up the stairs into the bathroom to take my sleeping pills, and into my bed. The sweetness of his smile shifted my heart painfully, stirring memories long buried. Only rarely did I think of my dead brother, and then when I could not help it. Like now, thirty-five years later, taken unawares by Adam Barowski and the surfacing of the past during the Polish mass. Adam Barowski was beginning to get to me, but now it was too late.

I had walked away from any concept of a God when I was thirteen, a long-legged desolate adolescent forced from my dreams by the politicians into learning Latin through the medium of the Irish language. I had turned the intrinsically difficult task of translating Latin into Gaelic into a game of revenge, and soon excelled in the vaguest, wildest translations, for which the authorities had to give me credit. Adam Barowski and the Second World War were far away then. De Valera, the taoiseach, kept Ireland out of it. The only good thing he ever did for the country, Mr Loughnane the butcher said. De Valera refused to let the English use the seaports, a fact I supported and defended at English cocktail parties in London twenty-five years later. Not everyone wanted the English to win the war. Mr Loughnane the butcher said he hoped the Krauts would wipe the English off the face of the earth, and if he hadn't ten children to feed he'd go over and give them a hand. The English accused de Valera of hiding German submarines in the Irish harbours, but he denied it. Sister Immaculata, who had a moustache and a radio down on her pig farm, said the accusation was pigswill and she wished politicians had a fraction of her pigs' intelligence. Look at what the Brits had done, said Mr Loughnane. Letting that murderous rabble, the Black and Tans, out of the jails lead by that blackguard Oliver Cromwell, to shut the Irish up, when everybody who was anybody knew that nobody could shut the Irish up. A Black and Tan soldier had fallen in love with my mother Mary Rafferty, but Delia had called him a cockroach assassin and ordered him off the property with a horsewhip. Delia was famous for that as well as her homemade butter. I drifted into a drugged sleep before long. Living in the past can sometimes be a cure for the present.

Chapter Ten

THE PRIEST

I was wakened next morning by Disraeli patting the top of my head.

"Dial 999," I said.

"What for?" he whispered.

"The house is on fire," I said.

"It is not on fire. Visitors are here. Me and Malachy didn't like to wake you up."

"At this ungodly hour?"

"It's twelve o'clock nearly."

"What visitors?"

"Father Joe and the National Front."

"What do you mean the National Front?"

"Hilda Uphill."

"You're joking."

"I'm not joking."

I scrambled out of bed and we went across into the

bathroom. I swigged Listerine out of the bottle to freshen my mouth, rinsed it around and spat it out. I scrubbed my face with a wet face towel.

"Tell them I have a headache. Tell them I'm not well."

Disraeli sat disconsolately on the edge of the bath, flicking his catapult at Fred who was sitting proudly with my slipper in his baby jaws.

"Sometimes you drink too much," Disraeli said.

"I have not been drinking, and it's very rude to call Mrs Uphill the National Front," I said and brushed my teeth.

I didn't need trouble from Disraeli just then. He followed me into the bedroom as I zipped up jeans and buttoned a shirt.

"She is the National Front, and worse than Albert. They think the blacks should be sent home to the jungle and the Irish to the bogs."

"Who told you that?"

"Malachy told me."

So Malachy was the source of Disraeli's precocious cynicism which could come across as quaint and even amusing in a child of his age. I had lost my grip on what was happening in the children's world.

"For God's sake, don't cry until I come back, Disraeli. Tom and Lydia will be home soon."

I crossed the landing and went down the stairs. No wonder there was fighting in the schoolyards.

The Reverend Father Joseph Drumghoule and Hilda Uphill were ensconced on chairs at the window. Sitting in silence, they were socialising by accident and not by design by the look of them. The craggy-faced, black-headed Irishman and the blonde English Rose were an unlikely pair. Joe's spectacles were halfway down his long nose, which as I knew from experience could mean he was up to mischief. We all spoke at once.

"Hi, Father Joe. Hi, Hilda," I said.

"Is the back any better, Brigid Mary?" asked Joe.

"Why there you are, Brid," said Hilda.

I lowered myself on to a high chair near the door.

"Getting better," I said.

"The colour is gone from your face," said Joe.

We sat waiting for someone to speak first. I shifted as the bubble of pain intensified in my spine.

"I believe you have a bad back, Brid. You must try Shiatsu," said Hilda.

"I have taken the liberty of raiding your cupboard," said Joe.

A bottle of Irish whiskey stood uncorked on the sideboard, and two empty glasses stood on occasional tables beside the guests.

"As we are gathered together on this grand spring morning, it behoves me well to make Gaelic coffee, as a welcome out of the hospital," Joe said in his pulpit voice.

He went out, leaving me looking enquiringly at Hilda, wishing Joe to be quick with the whiskey.

"I am sorry you have been kept waiting, Hilda. Disraeli has a problem."

"Everybody has a problem," said Hilda.

So much for Disraeli and his problem.

"I came to thank you for obliging me at the Taverna Polonia and to ask if you will do it for a few weeks?"

"Out of the question, I'm afraid," I said.

I spoke in a voice which would brook no argument, but my heart missed a beat.

"I have no option but to be truthful, Brid. Adam Barowski is within his rights to refuse payment unless I cover my contract, and I need that money."

"Cover your contract then."

"Albert is suspicious. It's too dangerous."

"Suspicious of what, may I ask?"

"Suspicious I am having an affair with Adam."

"You must try elsewhere. I cannot help you any more."

I busied myself with cigarettes and lighter. I did not want to look at her face. I could hardly believe what I had heard. Was the woman having an affair or not? I didn't want to know. In any case, what was to stop her denying it to Albert, whether there was anything in it or not, and continuing to work out her contract? Unless she had been rejected and it was wishful thinking. I felt a weight lift off me. Surely I had not totally misread the interest in Adam's eyes across the Mirski's dinner table.

Joe, with a towel across his serving arm, swung into the room with a tray of Gaelic coffee. Hilda stood up, straightening her short, accordion-pleated skirt, which was common as mud in my opinion and worn mostly these days by working-class day trippers from the North.

"I must leave you both to it. I know you won't refuse a second Gaelic coffee, Father Drumghoule. I'll give you time to reconsider, Brid. Don't trouble to see me out."

We took her at her word.

"Intermission time, and round one to Mrs Uphill. What is this about a cablegram, Brid?"

"Stanley is alive in Africa, is to come in the summer or I am to go there."

"Wow. No wonder your back seized up. Where is the cablegram?"

He pushed his spectacles up his nose and put the cream-topped drink beside me. I unzipped my bag and gave it to him.

"I'd not have thought psychiatry would have much place in the Sudan now. War can empty the mental hospitals; impending death can cure neurosis. How do you feel?"

"Like a lobster without its shell."

"And Malachy?"

"Confused. Glad his father is alive and betrayed by the years of silence. He has gone quiet. I guess we did not expect to hear from him again."

Fred scratched and bayed like a grown-up hound outside the door. Disraeli came in with the puppy. He was crying.

"Malachy won't talk to me," he said.

Joe held his arms out, took Disraeli on his knees.

"Blow," he said, and held out his handkerchief. "Crushed is the spirit of the brave Disraeli, and the girl from Galway is sick of soul. Come out to the garden."

I was sick of soul, but not only from the cablegram and the long silence before it. I was sick from the images of Hilda together with Adam in my head. Where would it all end? In tears, Mary Rafferty would have said, for the way of the transgressor is hard. Maybe so, I thought defiantly, but what had that to do with me, the victim and not the transgressor? Some victim, said my inner saboteur. A married woman, entertaining the deadly sins of envy and lust, not counting the pride and the anger.

The three of us sat on the hammock while Joe swung us back and forth with his long legs. The April sun shone fitfully in a mackerel sky, and low-wheeling seagulls flashed silver in its light. The air was fragrant with spring smells, the hawthorn tree festooned in white, the cherry tree covered with balls of pink puffs, the baby buds about to unfold on the laburnum tree. A chill wind blew up, tossing the tree branches, rippling and waving the uncut grass. Joe took off his jacket, and placed it about my shoulders.

"There is a storm at sea, my friends; the seagulls are in from the shore," he said.

"I want fish and chips," said Disraeli.

"My bag is inside, my love," I said.

"A man cannot think on an empty stomach," said Joe, giving him a handful of silver.

"Be careful on the crossing, my love," I told the sad child.

Disraeli went down the garden path and out the gate, shutting Fred inside. Fred raised his head to howl, thought better of it and came to my lap for consolation. I was glad of something warm and alive to hold.

"The old brown thorn-trees break in two high over Cummen Strand," Joe recited.

"Go on," I said.

Under a bitter black wind that blows from the
   left hand;
Our courage breaks like an old tree in a black
   wind and dies,
But we have hidden in our hearts the flame out of
   the eyes
Of Cathleen, the daughter of Houlihan.

Tears rose inside me, and he sensed my grief and wrapped an arm around me. He held me firmly until the spasm passed. We sat in silence a long time, and I drew solace from the enchanted lines of William Butler Yeats and the arm of my old friend.

"I see your father in you at times, Brid. He had the hidden flame."

"My mother gave me anxiety masquerading as love."

"Let your mother rest in peace. Her heart was in Shane's grave."

"And what about me?"

"So was yours."

I did not deny it.

"The cablegram was posted on St Patrick's Day. He thought of you then."

"It is too late to think of us."

"I thought at first it was another woman, or that he had cracked up. Psychiatry is a hard field to work in. But then you would have seen those coming."

"I saw nothing."

"Maybe, my girl from Galway, you were not looking."

It was said with gentleness. It was not a rebuke.

"He will be a stranger now, and besides, I have met someone else."

Things were at a pretty pass when I was telling the priest about Hilda's leavings.

"Do I know him?"

"He's Polish. He took me to mass on Easter Sunday."

"To Devonia Church?"

"Yes. He sings in the choir."

"You'll be safe if he keeps on singing."

"He was at the Mirski's dinner party."

"And since?"

"The boys stopped him going to the hospital, and I've taken the phone off the hook."

"You can't keep that up. Is he free?"

"He has a ring on his right hand."

"And now you're not free."

"Don't preach at me."

"You know me better than that."

"Sod off."

"That's more like my Brid. St Michael defend me from stubborn women."

"Why should I be bound by church rules when I cannot comprehend God?"

"Accept the incomprehensibility of God by the mind, but not to experience and observation. Thomas Aquinas's five causes argument for the existence of God came from experience, observation, not theory, and it stands today. He saw God as the prime mover in a relatively stable system."

"Don't tell me the five causes now, for God's sake."

"I will not. Search and experience yourself."

"I have no time now."

"Make it. Life with God is great fun. Smell the rain on the wind and have faith for now."

"What is faith?"

"It's a gift. Ask for it and you'll get it."

> *For even though the fig tree does not blossom,*
> *nor fruit grow on the vine,*
> *even though the olive crop fail,*
> *and field produce no harvest,*
> *even though flocks vanish from the folds,*
> *and stalls stand empty of cattle,*
> *yet I will rejoice in the Lord.*

"That's all right for the likes of you with poetry in the soul. I envy you."

"You'd soon get over that if you saw what I have to put up with from some of the pious parish ladies."

"Nobody will answer the front door bell," shouted Anja Mirska, clambering over the garden fence.

"It's young Anja," said Joe.

"You know her?"

"I tried and failed to prepare her for confirmation. Devonia Church is too far away for her."

Anja's boots rang on the timber as she cleared the fence and came towards us. Joe got up and shook her hand.

"You get more beautiful every time I see you," he said.

"You should not tell lies with a dog collar on."

"Why do I never see you at church?"

"Because I'm not there, silly. I came to say I am sorry for being a bugger on Monday, Brid."

"I thought that was you at your best."

"Have you been smoking pot, young lady?" asked Joe.

"Who's been at the whiskey bottle then?"

There was room for the three of us on the hammock.

"Why are you like that with your parents, Anja?" I asked.

"It makes me mad the way she lets him walk all over her."

"Maybe she has chosen that way."

"She didn't choose to live in a hell hole of disapproval, and it's not her fault she has a scandalous daughter who won't go to medical school or that she got fat, cooking for him."

"Be angry, but not too long, little one," said Joe.

"I'm not little."

"Your father has lost a lot, and it's no good keeping them awake at night," he said.

"They will always find some bloody thing to keep them awake. Anyway, I am sorry for being rude, Brid. Pan Barowski fancies you."

I felt my face blush with pleasure, whether pure or impure I could not say.

"Is there a Mrs Barowska?" asked Joe.

"Dead from booze, they say."

"We are brave to live in a world full of people," I said.

"Thank God for God," said Joe, and began to sing as he loved to do. I joined in and felt uplifted at once. He had that effect on me.

> *Oh, the summer time is coming*
> *And the trees are sweetly blooming*

And the wild mountain thyme
Grows around the blooming heather.

Will you go, lassie, go?
And we'll all go together
To pull wild mountain thyme
All around the blooming heather,
Will you go, lassie, go?

People clapped from the bus queue over the fence.
"I must go now," said Anja.

"Me too," said Joe. "Pass me my flak jacket for confessions, love."

They left and I felt fragile without Joe's steadying influence. He made me feel that life was not meant to be taken so seriously, that it was fun. Sufficient unto the day was the evil thereof.

Chapter Eleven

THE SON

Like the rest of humanity who labour under the misapprehension that some days cannot spring another dirty trick, I found that the day was far from done. Somebody had replaced the handset on the telephone, and it rang, shrill, persistent, as I came into the house. I blamed Malachy for interfering with my domestic arrangements. It might stop if I ignored it. The terracotta tiled kitchen floor, a warm comfort to the eye normally, was hidden under trodden-in grease and food debris. Mindful of my vulnerable spine, I set about freeing the beautiful floor from its sticky mess, armed with a scraper, mop and bucket. The telephone continued to peal. I should have confiscated the telephone, hidden it. Brave I might be to live in a world inhabited by people, but even the most fearless of soldiers needed his barracks. Joe had said I could not keep the receiver off for ever, and might have replaced it out of whiskey-fuelled mischief, but it was a waste of time being cross with the priest. Joe could disarm me without even trying. I gave in, went into the hall and lifted the receiver and, would you believe it, it was Hilda Uphill.

"Brid, at last. Can I not persuade you to help me out?"

"Sorry. You must find someone else."

"I've already told you there is nobody else."

The tone of acerbity in her voice strengthened me. How dare she?

"You'll find a solution."

"I'd not have asked you if I had one."

"Tell Albert the truth. Tell him about your financial position."

"He'd kill me if he thought I was up to anything. I cannot."

At least poor Albert would have no trouble disposing of the body in his funeral parlour. I bet there were times he had considered it, handy as it was. I did not want to hear any more. I did not want her to mention Adam Barowski. Some things were best left alone.

"Excuse me now, Hilda, and I am sure something will work out for you."

I put the receiver down; it rang at once, and I picked it up angrily, ready to do battle, but it was him. The sound of his voice filled my startled mind like a loud waterfall, and I whispered, "Hello."

"Hello. I am glad you are out of hospital. Is your back better?"

"Improved, thank you."

"Your son said you were not allowed visitors. Are you free tonight?"

"Not really. Malachy is not well."

"May I ask what is wrong?"

"I am not sure."

The silence was uncomfortable.

"In that case, maybe you will allow me to call in a few days?"

Brought up to be polite, what could I do but acquiesce? But then I had been brought up not to lie either. I had used whatever was going on with Malachy to buy time before facing the Pole. Mendacity. No good ever came of it. No good did.

I dealt with the kitchen floor, sat with a cigarette and coffee and waited for the shining browns, blues and yellows of the earthen floor to comfort my soul. Adam had sensed I was backing off. I blocked out the image of him with Hilda by tackling the refrigerator, making food lists to replenish the food storage cupboards, as if preparing for a siege against an unknown enemy. I had done the same before the unexpected deaths of my parents, before the unexpected birth of Malachy three weeks before time. Precognition could be a curse as well as a gift. A contingency might not have to be dealt with at all. Mary Rafferty had believed in being prepared for the worst, unlike John who had the faith to allow things to take place in their own time. I flung the remainder of Fred's tinned food into a cupboard under the kitchen sink and determined to be more like my father.

But try as I might to emulate my father's peaceful nature during the day, sleep began to escape me at night.

I became frightened by the powerful opposing forces now catapulting me into a decision not to see the Pole again, and then to the opposite one in a matter of minutes. A rock-like decision to put him out of my life signposted to a destination without him. I soon softened into a kind of quagmire leading to the opposite path. Such vacillations made me fear for my sanity, and the morals instilled in my childhood heightened my confusion. I had not been so attracted to any man before. Dancing with Stanley had been fun, but as sex was the major deadly sin in the island of saints and scholars, it was also, as somebody said, the eleventh consideration when choosing a life partner. Nobody talked of fancying someone; nobody had heard of pheromones in those days. A remembered conversation heard in a Dublin bus between two men who would not see middle age again made me smile as I tossed and turned.

"A grand new wife you have, Michael."

"She's not too good in the legs, John."

"It's not for racing you want her. Won't she answer the rosary for you."

Dublin of the faith, the theatre of high romance, where the pinnacle of aspiration was a rising road, a child every year and death in Ireland.

Stanley might be the handsomer of the two men, but he grew heavy with the years, and a deeply carved frown line gave him a look of brooding severity, robbed him of the devil may care. Disconsolately I wondered about the part I played in that change, that propensity to irritability. I could imagine Barowski being menacing if crossed, but not irritable, as buoyant, as vital as he was. But then neither could I have imagined it of Stanley long ago. I tried to shift the guilt. Had I not done my best, had the best of intentions from the beginning? And it did not matter now whether Barowski had driven his wife to drink and bedded Hilda Uphill or not. Stanley was alive in the Sudan. I tried to control my jealousy by concentrating on the broken veins on Hilda's face. Nothing could be done about them but painting her face like a clown's. She must be fifty if a day, I thought venomously, conveniently forgetting I was not far off it myself. It would be comforting to think that she had seduced the Pole, but I knew that nobody could make him do what he did not want to do.

My problems were driven out of my head with the shock of Malachy's refusal to get out of bed to go to school. He turned his face to the wall and would not talk. I desperately wanted a whiskey before I called the doctor, but refrained. The doctor said there was nothing organically wrong. He would recover from the emotional shock sustained at the news from Africa given time and love. He could not say then how long it would take. Disraeli and Fred moped downstairs while the dreadful silent listlessness went on upstairs.

It was so unlike Malachy. He had never been a quiet child. His birth three weeks early had caused a furore. Would he be a breach birth or would he turn around in time? He waited until the staff were scrubbed up and ready for a Caesarian section, then confounded us all by swinging around and shooting head first into the world, greased like a long distant swimmer. As if he could have done it any time he felt like it. No anaesthetic or steel forceps for him. Stanley was delighted with his healthy strong son even if he did have the Rafferty red hair. It was obvious that this new person who had not come in by the door, now gazing with cosmic wisdom at the ceiling lights, was the new thinker in the Finucane family.

What was going on with him now? His silence, his listlessness, so unusual for him, was a spectral energy. He had always fought for what he wanted, from the time he had objected with lung power to the rules of the hospital, like feeding by the clock and removal from me at night. Visiting time was a shambles. His loud protestations at the horizontal position woke the other babies, stopped the visitors' conversations. Noisy and rambunctious, he was a party baby, angelic in a room full of people, liking being passed around in the noise and the smoke, as long as nobody sat down too long with him. He was a star turn at cocktail parties, trading places with the canapés, the fags and the bags, cracking the veneer of what passed for conversation. He did not like it when everyone went home and he no longer the centre of the universe. He slept only when tired from the excitement of his life.

Now fifteen years later, he had gone quiet, was beginning for the first time in his life to sleepwalk at night. He put the heart across me when I saw him coming down the stairs, his eyes fixed and blind. I had heard it was unwise to wake a sleepwalker, so I watched in horror in case he might fall. He stood still in the hall, head alert as though listening, and lifted the latch. I followed as he entered the sitting room. His dark silhouette framed by the moonlit window could have been that of Stanley, head turned, waiting. I had not realised he had grown so tall, broadened so much at the shoulders. Trembling, I followed him as he climbed the stairs, lay on his bed still asleep. I covered him with a duvet. My nightcap of whiskeys did not work. I did not sleep until dawn, when I dreamed I was on my honeymoon with Stanley. He had poured Napoleon brandy all over me, and I was disappearing as he licked it off inch by inch.

I warned Disraeli about the nocturnal trips, but he knew already. I heard the church bells peal three times that night and got up to see Malachy, Disraeli and Fred sitting on the monk's bench in the hall. Malachy's eyes were open, blind. Disraeli signalled hush. Fred shivered mournfully, making no sound. I returned to bed, drank some whiskey and waited, but I soon fell into an exhausted sleep without hearing them come up the stairs. I had a terrible nightmare. I saw my father die in defeat, eyes blazing with disappointment at the loss of his life. I rang Joe at seven o'clock next morning. I did not know what it was he could do, but I could no longer cope on my own.

Twilight had gathered the four corners of the sky and was shaking the light out of it when Joe came, apologising for being delayed. Going straight up to Malachy's room, he asked not to be disturbed. I watched television with Disraeli and Fred with the sound turned down in case the priest called, but he did not, and much later I put them to bed in the guest room. The tick tock of the swinging pendulum in the hall clock sounded loudly over the rain-laden wind swishing mournfully through the trees in the darkness outside. When Joe came down he looked haggard, pale, inward looking.

"Malachy will be all right. Healing has worked for him, and can work again," he said.

"How can you tell?" I asked.

"The energy came out of me and felled him to the floor."

"Is he hurt?"

"I caught him, but the fall never hurts. He rested a long time. Let him sleep now."

"Katy Quinn said you had the gift of faith healing. Whiskey?"

"Thanks. Tell her to keep that to herself. Some are born with the gift, others can develop it. When I was two, I put my hands on a dying sheepdog's head. He licked my face and lived for years."

"Is that what is called faith healing then?"

"I find that a misnomer. Babies and animals have no faith as such. Neither have they hostility to block the energy. Energy can transform matter, as matter can be transformed into energy. It's a reverse process, that's all, but it's unpredictable."

Stanley had dismissed healing as a relic of pre-scientific superstition, and I had agreed with him. I poured the whiskeys while Joe sat and lit his pipe.

"How do you know it's worked for Malachy then?"

"My experience tells me."

"Will it last?"

"I repeat if necessary."

"How do you know it will work the next time?"

"If it works once it can work twice. Keep this to yourself or I'll have no peace."

We finished the drinks and he left. I went up to

Malachy's room. He was asleep on his back, his fists thrown up like a baby. I felt the atmosphere to be strangely and powerfully charged, and it frightened me. Something I did not understand had gone on, was still going on as far as I knew. My rational mind had heard Joe's explanation, but that meant nothing to me as I stood petrified beside my sleeping child. Before I slept the sound of Chopin's "Nocturne" came drifting through the walls. Could Mr Pocock be serenading me, playing the piano at this hour of the morning? Did the man ever sleep at all?

Chapter Twelve

HIATUS

I tried to live in the day, taking on the role of a house-proud woman to take my mind off the frantic anxiety I felt as I waited to see if Malachy improved. I forced myself to be too busy to hover around him, and out of the corner of my eye I saw him gradually lose the dreadful empty look and begin to eat. I had let the cleaner go after Stanley left, to avoid questions about my lone state, and I began with the lavatories, upstairs and downstairs. They benefited from my burst of activity, and so did the garden. I bought a bottle of Dot lavatory cleaner and disinfectant to begin with, but as one bottle of wine was never enough, one bottle of Dot seemed not enough either, and I found myself buying a second bottle of New Improved Fragrant Sanilav lavatory cleaner, which not only killed germs and kept toilets fresh, but also removed limescale, which must be a terrible thing to have in a toilet bowl, it looked so important on the label. The family deserved full protection in those hard times. I didn't know whether limescale lurked in the lavatory bowls or not, but it could well be under the rims, where I had never looked in my life. Masked and gloved I spent the morning on my knees at the lavatory bowls with a scrubbing brush. Limescale lurked indeed, and either the Sanilav lied or years of neglect had cemented the deposit beyond chemical intervention, for I had to scrape it off with the breadknife which would need disinfecting before lunch. Afterwards I had a bath sprinkled with essential oil of geranium to stabilise the emotions and wondered to whom I could show off my immaculate lavatories. Nobody came to mind except Hilda Uphill who claimed that she could tell a woman's character by her front doorstep, and I was not having her.

The afternoon sky filled with mare's tails, tufts turned down, which grandmother Delia claimed to be an ill boding. Was Malachy going to be all right? I wondered if Disraeli was beginning to settle down with his parents. If he had forgiven them. He still came daily to visit us and sometimes stayed the night since Malachy got sick. Tom and Lydia said time would heal and let him stay with us when he wanted to. They understood everything as they always had done. I drew the curtains on the darkening sky, pulled the ceiling light down over the kitchen table, and served sausages and mash in the comforting pool of light.

"Them pills is making me dizzy, Mom," said Malachy.

"Those pills is making you dizzy," corrected Disraeli.

"Keep taking them until I call the doctor," I said.

Maybe he could come off the pills soon. Maybe he didn't need them any more.

"Who's teaching you English grammar, boys?" I asked.

"Miss O'Casey," said Malachy.

"Miss Patel," said Disraeli.

I chewed my sausage. and wondered if I should tell the police to take Stanley off the missing persons list. If the news spread I would be faced with embarrassing questions. Let him stay on the list with the hordes who felt there were worse things in life than homelessness. I heard loud banging on the wall from Mr Pocock's house next door and I felt afraid. Doors would have to be locked in future.

That night I got out of bed and fearfully crossed the landing into Malachy's room, where the red glow of the night light shone on the three occupants of the bed. Disraeli and Fred were back in the bed with Malachy. That was a good sign. Disraeli slept with his head stuck in Fred's fat stomach, and Malachy was on his back, hands flung up on the pillow, his face peaceful. My heart faltered. Joe had said the unconscious of a sleeping child was open to prayer, and I asked for healing energy for Malachy, for Disraeli so bravely hiding his separation pain.

I had believed my father when he said that God could do things impossible for man, like drawing a straight line. He told me the edge of a razor blade was a wobbly line under a microscope, unlike the dead straight lines of the geometric patterns of frost on the window pane in midwinter. What a lot I had missed by closing my mind and my ears to my father's lovely world when I was twelve, but how privileged to have known him at all. I imagined him in his study, regarding me gravely as I sat on the window seat looking out at the cow grazing pasture, the cascade of white flowers on the horse chestnut tree.

"Will I see Adam Barowski again, Dad?"

"What does your soul say, Brigid Mary?"

"Maybe I have no soul, Dad."

"Every mortal has a soul, Brigid Mary."

"Mine is asleep or dead."

"The soul neither sleeps nor dies."

"It's deliberately silent then."

"It is clear that the silence asks you to do nothing."

"Nothing at all?"

"Nothing at all."

His smile was the intolerably sweet smile of his dead son Shane and his soul-sick grandson Malachy. The smile of the patient father showing me how to tie my shoe laces, showing me the intricacies of geometry, algebra and physics as I grew up. I went back to bed and slept for what was left of the night, like a good child.

Dawn brought with it a storm, and I was wakened by a loud clap of thunder and gales of wind. Was the house safe? Were the children safe? The boys came running and Fred shot under the bed as forked lightning zigzagged down the sky and hit the distant hills.

"God is moving the furniture in the sky," shouted Disraeli.

"Thunder travels one mile a minute. Count to the next clap and see where the storm is," shouted Malachy.

They counted to fifteen.

"Fifteen miles away," yelled Disraeli. "It's a hurricane."

"It's forked lightning," I said.

"What's forked lightning?" Disraeli asked, and I didn't know.

"Ground positive electricity meeting negative space electricity," said Malachy.

"Can it kill?" Disraeli asked.

"Yep. Forked can. Sheet lightning goes back into the clouds," said Malachy.

Malachy's schooling, never mind the grammar, could be taken off the list of worries which kept me awake at night.

The tall cypress trees at the side of the house did a crazy belly dance, top branches waving wildly at the sky, middle branches shimmying and shivering. The rogue wind stripped the blossoms and leaves off the trees down the avenue and flung them up in the air in a wild riot of colour like a carnival. Whatever saint had said God was no pussy cat was right. Incomprehensible, an X factor, but no pussy cat. My hands shook with fear. Pray, Sister Marie Louise had said. To the X factor?

"We have to put up a lightning conductor, Mimmo," said Malachy. Disraeli pulled the squeaking Fred from under the bed and cuddled him to an occasional whimper.

"I'll think about it tomorrow," I said.

Nothing like danger for focusing the mind. Safety for myself and the children was uppermost in my racing mind. Neither Adam nor Stanley mattered to me then. Spotless lavatories lost whatever importance they might have had. Loud thunder and forked lightning grounded me.

"Why does Fred hate cracking noises?" asked Disraeli.

"It's like gunshot," said Malachy.

"He never heard gunshot," said Disraeli reasonably.

"It's like snapping of branches by the big cats in the forest."

"He never heard them either."

"It's his survival instinct. It's atavistic," said Malachy.

"What's atavistic?" asked Disraeli, as they went down to breakfast.

"Oh God, ask Mimmo," said Malachy.

I pretended not to hear. I was not sure what atavistic was either. I began to cook rashers, eggs and black puddings. The early morning smell of my childhood. I never put the extractor on for that. Disraeli sat with Fred behind the sitting room sofa, and Malachy came into the kitchen.

"I'm coming to Africa with you."

"It may not come to that."

"The Hadendua tribe is dangerous. They are in the mountains by the Red Sea. The Brits call them the Fuzzy Wuzzy."

"I wouldn't be going to the mountains."

"You might have to."

My hands still shook as I cooked. The raging force of the storm began to abate. The wind still keened around the house, but the lightning flashed less often, and the thunder sounded further away.

"I wouldn't take unnecessary risks, Malachy. Life is the most important thing in our lives."

I spent time in the garden, feeling the lift of late spring in the earth as I planted cuttings of *Hydrangea petiolaris* along the sunless north wall of the house. Birds flocked around the bird feeder in the garden. Wrens, thrushes, sparrows, blackbirds and a red-breasted robin were daily visitors, filling the air with birdsong, uplifting my spirit until anxiety, a cunning interloper, would catch me unawares. Would Malachy be all right? Was I going to get rid of Barowski now that Stanley was back in the picture? Did I want to? What would I do about Stanley? Was Joe the right person to ask how prayer worked, if it worked? Supposing he had a simple faith and didn't know?

Days stretched in slow motion, punctuated by times of mental turmoil when I drank whiskey and bursts of physical activity when I left the drink alone. The garden began to flourish like a well-loved English garden, with its mowed lawn and tidy bushes, and the house took on a new lease of life with shining floors, walls and white woodwork. Busy as I was, I managed to nod at Mr Pocock across the garden fence. I even felt a fleeting compassion for him because his eyes didn't join in when he smiled. I had never enquired about his life, afraid to give him an opening, but had I felt any attraction towards the man I would have been friendly. I was very friendly to Adam Barowski when he rang to ask if Malachy was getting better and was glad to tell him he was back to his usual self. When you got down to the nitty-gritty of it, it was all down to sex between men and women. I thought about that as I removed a drink circle off the mahogany coffee table with methylated spirit and linseed oil. Joe said the final commandment to love one another was the answer to the problems on the planet, but mankind was not ready to take it on. Unless everybody else was doing it, I was not prepared to try. People would think you were oversexed or soft in the head. I had not risked it with Stanley, and I was going to have to watch out with Barowski. The front door bell rang. I was shocked to find Adam Barowski in a camel hair coat, standing on the doorstep with a bouquet of flowers.

"Good day to you, Brid. May I come in if it's not inconvenient?" he said, bowing, kissing my hand. "I thought, as Malachy is better, you could come with me to the Posk, the Polish Social Centre, tonight."

He walked past me into the hall.

"Let me put the flowers in water."

"Your back seems better."

I busied myself arranging the flowers on the sofa table near the window to catch the light.

"Thank you. Where on earth did you find the wild flowers? Primroses, cornflowers, Jacob's ladder."

"You have been avoiding me, Brid," he said.

"And foxgloves," I said.

"The woods are full of wild flowers. Did you hear what I said?" he asked.

I walked to the fire and kicked the logs wrapped in the flames.

"You don't deny it?"

I stared at the spitting logs.

"Why are you afraid of me?" he asked.

"I am not afraid of you," I said.

"You noticed my wedding ring. Did you think that Zofia would set you up with a married man?"

I felt my face pinken and kept a stubborn silence.

"My wife died ten years ago. I intend to marry again," he said.

"I don't know the first thing about you, nor you about me," I said.

"I know enough, and time can remedy the rest," he said.

He came to me and took my hands, but I broke away from him, rummaged in my bag and handed him the cablegram from Stanley. His expression did not change as he read it.

"And what is that to us?" he said.

"He is my husband and Malachy's father," I said.

"He is neither. You can divorce him immediately for desertion."

"I married for life, for better or worse."

"Dog's blood. He walked out of your life without a word. Divorce is mandatory when a marriage is over in my view."

"He must have had his reasons."

"You had a right to the truth. No wonder your son was sick. Years of silence and now this rubbish telegram."

"Maybe he didn't know the truth."

"Jesu Maria, give me patience. Tonight you must come with me."

"I am not sure I can leave the boys."

"You must find a less feeble excuse, Brid. I'm sure you have a babysitter."

His strong-toothed smile was as wry as his tone of voice, but as he bowed, a thick lock of hair fell across his face, and my resolution to stay away from him wilted and died.

"I'd like you to meet the boys first, if you don't mind," I said.

"I'd be delighted."

I called Malachy and Disraeli, and they came running down the stairs, into the room and looked with curiosity at the Pole.

"I'd like you to meet Mr Barowski, boys. He wants to know if I'll go to a concert tonight."

They shook hands politely.

"Would you allow me to take Mrs Finucane to a concert this evening, boys?"

"You can if you like," they both said together and backed out of the room.

"They are fine fellows. Can you get a sitter?" he asked.

"That is not a problem."

"I will call, with your permission, at seven o'clock," he said and left without ascertaining the said permission.

Going up the stairs, I decided I would do as Dad had said. I would just go along with it all. I rang Katy Quinn, who was glad to see the back of Patrick Quinn and the kitchen sink for the night. I was to enjoy myself and stay as long as I liked. She would sleep in the guest room as usual. Beethoven's "Moonlight Sonata" sounded sadly from next door. Mr Pocock was in from the garden and back at his piano. Maybe he would become famous in the music world, marry late in life. A late starter in some walks of life, unlike the rest of us, the exhausted from living already.

Chapter Thirteen

THE RED DRESS

I had been trained in my youth to dress modestly at all times but especially around men, who were easily excited and had little or no control over their sexuality. Poor men were weak in that department and could not be held responsible for moral lapses. It was always held to be the girl's fault when matters got out of hand, which they did with worrying frequency, resulting in hasty weddings or flights to England for baby adoption or the desperate last resort of abortion. It was thought to be lacking in sensibility or, not to put too fine a point on it, flagrantly whorish to display certain parts of the female anatomy before men. So how come I was toying with the idea of wearing the red dress that evening?

Stanley had quite liked me to wear the red dress to the occasional medical party, where it helped to knock some of the inevitable starch out of the evening. I sometimes wore it as a challenge to the dreaded cocktail parties, where I was expected to stand for hours in high heels, bag in hand, fag in hand, canapé in hand, drink in hand, holding forth in verbal cross-fire with persons never seen before and hopefully never again. Thankfully such parties were confined to an annual event resulting, as often as not, in spitting rows in the kitchen. A bright rationalisation made by a nerve-wracked hostess, unsteady already from gin ("Why have two when one will do?") left me with the lasting impression that hospitality was not the hallmark of the Home Counties. In the red dress, Stanley said I could be depended on to raise the collective blood pressure of the men and the savage jealousy of the more insecure women present. At the very least he expected me to cause a stir, and I was happy to oblige him, for if I had to suffer, why not them? I would not have been let in the doors if my wicked state of mind were apparent, but I was a good actress, and drink was a facilitator. Was this why I was thinking of wearing the red dress? To stir things up between myself and Barowski? Precisely. I was about to let the devil take the hindmost, to live and pay later. In hindsight I sometimes thought I would do the same again, but that was much later of course, when the worst of the pain had passed.

The boys thought I should go. I drank a finger of whiskey to steady myself and took trouble with my appearance. False eyelashes widened and darkened my eyes in a porcelain painted face with a glossy orange mouth, and hot rollers made my hair spring around my head in ringlets and tendrils, like Cleopatra bent on seduction. John Rafferty would turn in his grave, and it was unthinkable what Mary Rafferty would do. What after all was life without dressing up for an occasion? "And what about your husband, Madame?" said my inner saboteur over the banisters as I stood in the hall putting on my silver fox jacket. "Adultery ain't no joke." God couldn't have a cockney accent.

"Aw, shut up," I said.

Full of bravado I answered the front door bell and saw at once that I was not the only reprehensible reprobate. Adam Barowski meant business in the Polish colours, with a white dinner jacket, red tie and carnation, white calfskin shoes like the Polish pope. I was a sight for sore eyes, but helpless as a pinned-down butterfly before the unfathomable smile as he bowed and kissed my hand. Strapping myself into the car seat, I noticed the silver hair and beard were newly trimmed, the sideburns cleverly shaved on the bias. He pulled the heavy car out into the evening traffic. The sinking sun gilded stone, brick and treetops as he drove with authority to the Posk in the evening stillness.

"I like your perfume."

"Thank you."

A sensual man interested in the pursuit of pleasure.

"The Polish president, Wojciech Jaruzelski, ordered the crucifixes off the school walls today."

"Will they do it?"

"Not a chance. The Kremlin needs to do homework on the Polish character."

Perhaps I would need to do the same.

The Posk was a splendid building, another wild gesture of extravagance. I was glad to be dressed up, for the

Poles clearly attached importance to their attire, the foyer crowded with elegant people, the atmosphere that of a grand occasion. The Mazowse, a world renowned song and dance company, was the attraction.

The performance was a whirl of acrobatic dancing, choral and solo singing, both rousing and haunting. Colourful folk costumes depicted the different districts of their land, with boots stamping, fur hats flying, lace dresses, striped aprons swirling, white-breeched, flat-hatted men from the Tatra Mountains dancing, leaping, swinging mountain axes. Full-throated choirs contrasted with the startling purity of soloists so small in stature yet filling the great auditorium with sound. It was a kaleidoscope of an exuberant, unquenchable spirit, and the final pageant with every performer on the stage brought the audience to its feet, clapping and crying unashamedly. Slow tears coursed down the face of my companion, and I found myself crying with him. Maybe it was only in England that big boys did not cry. Curtain call followed after curtain call, for the people did not want them to go, taking the heart of their lost country with them, leaving them, the refugees, behind. Barowski had wisely booked a table for the dinner dance, for people crowded the restaurant, not wanting to leave the magic of the Mazowse behind. "Wesolego Alleluia", the Easter greeting, rang around the tables, and I was happy to let him order the food off the Polish menu. *Farmouszka*, a soup of beer, sour cream and cottage cheese served with croutons, was an adventure, as was the Cracowian duck and barley sauce. After a glass of brandy, he smiled into my eyes, and I was saddened that more than half his life was gone and I could never be part of it. The dark circles, the barometer of his emotional life, were pronounced.

"Do you go back to Poland?" I asked.

"Not these days. Last time I was asked to spy, so the Home Office prevents me. In any case I want to live."

He inspected the palm of my hand.

"You have a long life line, like me. We watch, we wait, and spring a Polish pope to rattle them."

"Tell me about Katyn Forest."

"It is not for the dinner table. You should know only that 15,000 Polish officers were silenced with sawdust in the mouth and shot in the back of the head there. The Kremlin will find out that the Pole is like a radish. Scrape off the red, and you find white inside. May I have the honour of this dance and all the others if your back won't suffer."

My back did not suffer. The ethnic orchestra of violin, piano accordion, double bass and drums was persuasive, and before the night was out, I danced the *polonaise*, the *mazurka*, the *oberek*, the *kujawiak*. I had no difficulty following my partner through the folk dances, for while they were more stately, more wildly athletic than those of my country, it was not for nothing I had won medals for step dancing in my youth. The dancers were entranced with each other, the rapture infectious, but elegance was maintained. Men mopped their brows, yet no dinner jacket was removed; the ladies were fit to drop from exertion, but cosmetics were constantly repaired. I fell in love with the Polish people that night for the sadness contained with such courage, gaiety and charm.

The Polish martial anthem, sung for a land they would never live freely in again, liquidation a fact for those who had tried, made me cry for them and for the sounds of my country: the pong of tennis balls from the quiet summer lawn, the piano from the parlour below, the ringing of the blacksmith's anvil.

We drove up through Hampstead, stopped beside the Round Pond, shaped like a hospital kidney dish, to watch two swans paying a seraphic visit. Barowski rolled down a window, and gusts of air fragrant with the smell of the yellow catkins of a pussy willow tree blew in. Dawn broke, throwing fiery tongues into the sky, and a nightingale sang from the woods. He asked if he could show me where he lived as we reached the heights of Highgate Hill, and it never occurred to me to decline. The fanlight over the front door of the narrow terraced house recalled the Georgian squares of Dublin. Prints of Dickensian London in the hall led into a half-timbered room with ground rugs scattered on gleaming bare boards. Embers smouldered in the fire grate; a lively John Bratby painting, *Still Life with Chip Pan*, with its cluttered kitchen table above it was a humourous slant on Barowski's present occupation. Long sashed windows looked out on a patio with elaborate trellis work and a red-berried tree. They rattled in a sudden surly wind, as rain spattered like bullets on the glass. He threw logs on the fire and poured champagne into tall goblets.

"You admire the mountain ash, Miss Finucane? It protects the house from the rumble of traffic and evil spirits."

We drank the champagne I should have refused on the mattress ticking sofa by the fireplace, and the bubbles went up my nose.

"May I ask if your marriage ever worked?" he asked.

"I don't know. I have no yardstick. I was lonely a lot," I said.

"Lonely for what?"

"I don't know."

"You don't talk about your brother."

"He is dead."

"Zofia told me."

"I prefer not to discuss that."

"Why not? Why not with me?"

He clasped my chin, forced me to look up at him.

"I never talked about it."

"Not to Stanley?"

"No."

"Did he try?"

"Once, before we married."

"Stand up, Miss Finucane."

He stood, pulled me up, put arms around me. After a while I had to ask for a handkerchief. His shirt front was wet with my tears. The champagne had been a mistake. He gave me his handkerchief.

"Blow," he said, as if to a child.

The lovemaking was a natural occurrence apart from some fumbling with clothes. It was as if we had know each other before, and this time I did not feel passed by. My innermost self was swept up into a quiet place of peace. We slept through what was left of the morning, damp heads together on the old goatskin rug. I was glad

it had not happened in a bed, a place of failure and loneliness to me. Perhaps he had known that. He knew a lot.
I scrambled into my clothes, examined my red face in the
bathroom mirror, and up sprang love like a cut-throat in
a back lane.

Chapter Fourteen

THE FUNERAL

"You better ring Mrs Mirska," said Malachy with his mouth full, as I came into the kitchen. "Katy went home this morning."

"Mrs Mirska rang two times and she was crying," said Disraeli from his high stool.

"It must be bad news," said Malachy.

"We looked in your bedroom," said Disraeli.

"But you were out," said Malachy.

"I stayed with friends," I said.

"What friends?" asked Malachy.

"Polish friends," I said, feeling flustered and defensive. The boys smiled conspiratorially at one another, and I left the kitchen before I lost my temper with them. I was not going to be made to feel guilty for attempting to live a life of my own. It was not their business where I had been or what time I had got in. I dialled Zofia's number.

"I am listening," said Zofia at once.

"Is anything wrong?"

"Bogdan died in his sleep. He was cold beside me this morning."

"Oh God. I'll come at once."

Whatever energy was undepleted by the night's activities drained from my body. What a thing. In the midst of life.

Bogdan Mirski's funeral was a grand sombre affair, even by Polish standards. These times were a crash course in that culture for me and a chastening reminder that my hard life was a privileged passage in comparison to other people's. Men stood to attention, white-banded arms raised in salute, war medals on their chests, as his coffined body was carried on the shoulders of his closest friends to the hearse. They closed ranks and marched in silence to the Polish church behind the hearse. Resplendent in his RAF uniform, Adam drove the black-veiled widow and daughter in the Daimler, while I drove by myself at the rear of the cavalcade. Candlelight illuminated the head of the old warrior in the open coffin at the altar, and people queued to demonstrate last respects by kissing the face. I could not bring myself to kiss a corpse now, as I could not kiss the stained face of my dead brother long ago. I had refused then, to the consternation of those about me, as I refused now, sitting ashamedly while people struggled by me. While I was not as accustomed to death as these poor people were, I began to recognise that I had lived a cowardly half-life, terrified of the long shadow of death while pretending it did not exist. I had lived as a shivering denizen of a twilight world, demanding love and afraid to give it. I felt unfit to be among these brave people. They began to recite the rosary in their mother tongue, and I sat at the back of the church watching the bent heads; not one of them, on the outside looking in, as I had been most of my life. I had not expected to be back in this church ever again, and it seemed a lifetime since I had first come here with Barowski and been felled by the purity of his singing voice. The dark eyes of Christ Pantocrator in the ceiling appeared non-judgmental to me this time.

And so the old cavalry officer who survived incarceration in the Lubyanka jail was buried with the Polish Eagle and the Union Jack flags under his favourite linden tree. Afterwards people flocked to the house and stayed for hours. I came to help with the never-ending supply of food and drinks and so, surprisingly, did Albert and Hilda Uphill, who didn't socialise with the Poles as far as I knew. Of course Albert was in the funeral business, and Hilda had worked in Polonia.

"Albert has found out," Hilda whispered desperately as, laden with plates of food, we passed one another in the hall.

"Found out what?" I asked, not waiting for a reply, as I swept into the crowded dining room.

Albert had either found out about Hilda's unpaid bills, her alleged affair with Barowski or both. Whichever it was, she looked worse than Zofia, the broken veins apparent on her cheeks. No man was worth that decline. The day continued like an Irish wake. There was no music, no dancing, but it was a party just the same. A celebration of Bogdan Mirski's life.

Foremost among the ageing and aged dignitaries attending were the Polish government in exile, among them Pan Kazimierz Sabbat, prime minister; Count Edward Raczynski, president, and Pan Roman Czerniaski OBE, minister for information. I noticed that Adam was completely at ease with these impeccably dressed old gentlemen, spending time with them in deep conversation and seeing that their glasses were filled. The snob in me attributed importance to his easy mixing with the upper classes, for I had as much right as anyone else to mix with the best. He introduced me to them as they stood in a privileged group around the fireplace, but not before pushing me up against a wall behind the scullery door and knocking the breath out of me with an enthusiastic embrace like the body-slap greeting of the jackal. As the vodka went down, the collective spirits went up, and the atmosphere lightened. As darkness descended, the curtains were drawn, and the toasts to a free Poland, to free elections in their annexed country began. Behind all the beautiful manners, the hand-kissing, heel-clicking, bowing and gallant flirting, they really thought of little else.

"What use is a government in exile?" I asked, as I washed glasses behind the bar in the hall.

"They have no choice," said Adam, throwing empty bottles in a bin. "They know they seem faintly ridiculous, refusing to face post-war reality. They know they raise derision in some quarters, but they don't care."

"Could they not go back and stand their ground?" I asked.

"The five percent who did were liquidated by the Russians. These men are unable to stop fighting for a free

Poland, even from Belgravia. They live for that, even though Churchill denied them recognition thirty-five years ago."

"Perfidious Albion," I said, halfway down another vodka.

"Expediency, fuelled by Russian champagne at the Yalta deal with Stalin forced him to do it," he said with more fair-mindedness than I was capable of.

I made my way into the crowded sitting room with a tray of glasses, collecting and distributing as I went. The minister for information with enough information to be going on with, I supposed drunkenly, had forsaken his privileged place at the mantelpiece and retired to an armchair where he continued to drink vodka and to twinkle at the ladies. I would not put it past him to be active with the ladies in private either, and he would never see eighty again. I would not put it past any of them actually. I had heard it said that the Poles were an energetic and childish people. Adam was now entertaining the room at large with a story about Stalin's failure to get Ernest Bevin, the foreign minister, to quell the dissident Polish voice from the meetings in Belgravia on Monday nights. Bevin had said that as they had not interfered with Karl Marx in the nineteenth century, they would not interfere with the Polish government in exile either. I did not see what was so hilarious about that. I caught Hilda swigging straight vodka from a bottle in the hall.

"Hilda, take it easy with that bottle."

"Don't be ridiculous. Everybody else is throwing it down like water."

I took the bottle from her.

"They are used to it. It's their custom," I said.

"Well, it's fast becoming mine," said Hilda, dabbing her mouth with a dishcloth.

I should have let the woman drink until she fell with the best china.

"You've had enough," I said.

"Look who's talking. And what about Albert? He's getting rat-faced."

Which he was, standing glassy-eyed among the dignitaries as if engrossed in their conversation of which he understood not a word. Indefatigable at drumming up business, Albert always said you never knew your luck. Relays of people had been fed luncheon and dinner, while the staff of the Polonia restaurant did the catering, and eventually I was seated between Adam and Pan Antoniewicz, his Battle of Britain co-pilot, as they talked in English for my benefit of the fifty operations, the 500 hours spent in the Coastal Bomber Command in Wellington aeroplanes. It was all the same to me whether they spoke in English or not.

I was keeping an eye on Zofia who could not be persuaded to leave the kitchen table and Anja who said she was fine, except for spraying her hair with bloody starch instead of hairspray. When Romanek put a cup of coffee in my hand, I was glad to escape upstairs to rest. I closed the door of Zofia's bedroom and sat on the pile of fur coats on the bed. There were at least a hundred people downstairs, and the noise came up like a muffled roar. Adam's eyes had not flickered in Hilda's direction, which should be reassuring but was not, for he would have known that I was watching him. Eyes in the back of his head. I felt light-headed and would have to see about my drinking when the funeral was over. I went out to the lavatory, where I heard sounds of vomiting from behind the bathroom door. Was it not too early for someone to be that drunk? The octogenarians were still upright in the sitting room. I waited in the landing and a white-faced Anja appeared.

"One too many, my dear?" I asked

"Since you ask, I am sick and tired of being sick and tired, and please don't broadcast it that I'm pregnant," Anja said going down the stairs, leaving me speechless.

She did not look pregnant, but then with her height and those clothes it wouldn't be obvious.

When the people who had travelled long distances— for distance was no deterrent to the Poles, like my own countrymen, when it came to funerals—had been fed, I was made to sit again at the table beside Adam, his co-pilot and the Polish government in exile. Steaming hot bigots, a stew of sauerkraut and spiced meats, was served by the staff of Polonia to sober up the guests who were taking leave. Conversation, translated by Adam, became urgent. Left to its own devices, Poland would put an end to the Communist Party, but the Kremlin would not allow it. Excitement rose in the discussions. Would Poland, so proud of her army, fight, better equipped as she was than Czechoslovakia? Would the Russian tanks roll in as they had in Hungary and Czechoslovakia ten years before? Would the West frown on intervention from Moscow and find ways of being disagreeable short of armed combat? There was hope behind the heated discussions, and I was excited and hopeful with and for them. With the toasts came the toast for the chivalrous life of Bogdan Mirski and to every Pole who had fought at home and abroad for a free Poland.

Count Raczynski stood up and announced it was time to leave, for the ladies deserved to rest. Slowly the people went away as the caterers began to clear up. I sent Zofia and Anja to bed, promising to come back next day. There was no sign of Hilda. She must have fallen foul of Albert or the drink or both. The dining room was deserted now except for some over-indulgent cavaliers asleep or unconscious at the tables. Romanek lit a new candle at the top of the table, brought brandy and coffee, and I sat smoking and drinking coffee with Adam, Antoniewicz and Roman.

"Adam will recite 'Pan Tadeusz' for Miss Brid in English," said Roman.

"It is too late," said Barowski, "and I am far from sober."

"It is never too late for Adam Miskiewicz," said Antoniewicz. "And I've seen you recite it less sober than you are now."

Adam arose and standing behind his chair, looked at the ceiling thoughtfully.

"I will try, in honour of Miss Finucane's presence among us and the memory of Bogdan Mirski," he said, and began to recite.

O, Mother Poland, thou are laid within the grave.
What men have power to speak of thee today?

How many memories, what grief unbroken,
for the land where servants more for masters dare
than wives for husbands otherwhere?
And where a soldier mourns his weapons, more
than sons their fathers over here.
And where they pour more tears,
and grief is longer, more sincere
for a dead dog, than a hero here.

Adam clicked his heels, bowed and taking his hand-kerchief from his breast pocket blew his nose with it.

"It is enough for now," he said.

The men sat with bowed heads in silence, then, tipsily wet-eyed, everyone clapped.

"Thank you for that." I laid a drunken hand on Adam's. I was near to tears myself.

I had made love with a man who had poetry in his soul for his lost land.

"The hope of liberation was kept alive by the poets and writers," said Roman, pouring fresh black coffee.

"We keep it alive today. A toast to the spirit of Bog-dan Mirski." Adam raised a glass, and the others fol-lowed suit.

After the unconscious cavaliers were aroused and everyone had gone, we walked to the front gate. Lilac was fragrant in the night air as we got into the Daimler. I had only really talked to Bogdan once, so why was I sad for the old soldier who would not be seen again in our midst? I was sad mainly for the part of Adam's life which was gone from me in the Poland I could never know or be a part of, no matter how hard I would try.

Next morning I awoke with a serious hangover and no recollection of the journey home. I'd had a blackout, and there was no telling in what condition Adam Barowski had left me. I wondered in horror whether the boys had seen me, whether he had had to undress me and put me to bed, and whether that was the last I had seen of him. Remorse and fear were my companions for the day.

Chapter Fifteen

THE COMMUNITY

I put Stanley's cablegram to the back of a stocking drawer, as if putting it out of sight could put it out of mind. What would happen if he did come? Maybe it was as well that Adam had seen me disgustingly drunk and had probably taken flight for good. I tried to banish that thought by busying myself in comforting the bereaved, visiting Zofia and Anja daily. The worst time was after the people left. Zofia, deprived of the purpose of her life in service to Bogdan, sat around listlessly. She lost her appetite and a lot of weight. One could catch glimpses of the slender girl she had been before she began sampling the rich Polish food her husband demanded. I was present when Anja chose to tell her mother that she was pregnant.

"You can't wear black at the christening, Mom," she said.

"What christening?" asked Zofia.

"I am three months pregnant."

"What is she saying, Brid?"

"She is telling you that you will have a grandchild in six months time."

"But she has no husband. There was no marriage."

"I don't want a marriage."

"You must marry at once. Who is the father?"

"He is not suitable."

"Jesu Maria. Are you mad? How could you let this happen?"

"It wasn't planned. It was an accident."

"Oh, Mrs Brid, can you believe it? What can we do with this generation? Should we not have beaten them more? You cannot keep this child, Anja. You will disgrace us in the community."

"Sod the community. Who are the community?"

"You must consider an abortion."

"Listen to the Catholic talking."

"Don't speak to me like that."

"Mother Teresa said nobody should be surprised at the state of the world when the women are killing their children."

Mother and daughter were not speaking to each other when I left, but at least Anja had come home. As the months passed, I persuaded Zofia that she couldn't live the life of her willful daughter and that after all it was a new life for the old one. Very gradually Zofia's character seemed to undergo a change. She had her faded fair hair permed and highlighted with blonde streaks. She bought and began to wear rather low-cut dresses and, most extraordinary of all, began to frequent the Polish church dances occasionally. Why not really? The poor woman needed taking out of herself. Who could expect her to sit at home and mourn night after night? Well, it seemed that the Polish community could and did. It was a flagrant flouting of their traditions for a widow to behave like that, and her husband not cold in the grave. She should not have been seen at any public function for a year, out of respect for the memory of her dead husband. She must have taken leave of her senses in her grief.

When Anja told me that her mother had taken a lover, even I was shocked. I who had no right to be shocked, sneaking out to make love with Barowski, for he had not taken flight after all. Perhaps he had taken my drunken state after the funeral to be a rare occurrence. Surely Anja was mistaken? She was not.

"I found them sitting up in bed drinking wine in the middle of the day. I told them to lock the sodding door in future. A musician, twenty years younger, and engaged to Marysia, our neighbour's daughter."

"Perhaps Zofia is ignorant of that."

"She knows. Marysia is at the dances where he plays the accordion. My mother says she wouldn't dream of coming between them. She says she can advise them about the marriage."

"Well, that is something, isn't it?"

"She is a liar, pretending to condone the marriage."

"Who may I ask is about to enter the blissful state of marriage?" said the Reverend Joe Drumghoule, coming in from the vegetable garden in his wellies.

I encouraged him to grow and sell vegetables for the pocket money to follow his beloved horses and get to the odd race meeting on his day off. He loved digging in the earth and watching things grow. He was a happy man.

"My mother's new boyfriend," Anja said, despite my warning glance.

Trained to keep his counsel unless asked for it, the priest let it pass.

Zofia seemed impervious to the rising consternation in the Polish community, which was set up like a mediaeval monastery to enable them to live apart from the host community. Nothing went unnoticed. I began to suspect that Zofia might even be enjoying the notoriety while hell-bent for destruction.

Those were exciting days for the Polish housewives. Phone bills rose with the consumption of alcohol and coffee. Of course, they had always known that Pan Bogdan had married beneath him. Everybody knew that. The community was composed of military officers, dentists, doctors, chemists, artists and their wives, and tolerated among them the odd artisan-gifted handymen who made a good living in the worlds of upholstery, decorating, building. Unless professional, the women did not go out to work and spent time competing with one another in their kitchens and their sitting rooms. They agreed that the fruit does not fall far from the tree, for look at the daughter, dressed like a gangster. So the telephones rang at all hours with the latest scandalous news of the mother and daughter, and it was the general concensus of opinion that it was as well that poor Bogdan had gone to meet his Creator when he did. The takings at the doors of the weekly church dances more than doubled, which no doubt pleased the priests even if the root cause of it could not.

Meanwhile Malachy seemed to be his old self and had gone back to school on Father Joe's advice. I kept an anxious eye on him and waited until he was asleep before sneaking out like a young girl to be with Adam for a while. Circumstances were forcing me into a clandestine love affair, and I was torn by divided loyalties. I wanted to warn Zofia that she was riding for a fall, to consider the young Marysia who was busy lining her bottom drawer for her trousseau, but I felt unfit to tell others how to conduct their lives. Was I not also riding for a fall if Stanley came in the summertime, and even if he did not? In any case Zofia would have heeded no warning, for she declared with dreadful coyness that Marysia a fool for thinking her an obstacle to the forthcoming wedding, when she intended to be a friend to them both, that is if it ever took place. For by now of course, the women had seen to it that Marysia was fully informed of what was going on. Adam had told me to keep out of it. I did not like the new Zofia as well as the old one, for the old serenity, the old fortitude, had gone, and in their place was a brittleness in her manner. Well, it was certainly going to end in tears, somebody's or everybody's, and I vacillated. "Do not interfere," I would think one day, flinging saucepans in a cupboard. The next day, swinging a tennis racquet at a carpet on the clothes line, I would worry how Zofia would survive her lover's forthcoming marriage if it took place as arranged, or the scandal in the Polish community if it did not. Zofia was in trouble no matter what happened, and I continued to worry, for it helped to keep my mind off my own dilemma. The Polish community watched and waited with bated breath, and I decided to take Adam's advice and do nothing. Later, of course, I was sorry.

Eventually, the worst happened, for Zofia's lover Jurek got married without telling her beforehand. A Polish neighbour had taken it upon himself the night before to enquire whether she was going to the wedding and spread the news of her reaction with relish. White as a sheet she had gone, had to sit down and burst into tears. Zofia and Anja were the only uninvited people in the community. Zofia wept and drank whiskey around the clock. It was the talk around the tables at the wedding reception. A triumph for the community. Jurek got off scot free. A young man sowing his wild oats, after all, and she who should have known better had got her deserts. I blamed Adam for not telling Zofia, booked as he was to sing at the wedding, but he said it was up to Jurek, no use coming from anybody else. Zofia refused to answer the telephone, closed and locked her front door, shut out her ruined life in the community. She committed an emotional suicide, or was murdered, depending on how one looked at it. Sadly, whichever it was, Zofia's gallant foray into what she thought was life was over. The message was not lost on me, I can tell you. You conformed or you were ostracised. The power of the Polish community was lethal. Had Adam looked at the consequences of bringing a Gael into that society?

Surely he must realise what the women would do to me, never mind to him. I would have to learn the language, the cuisine. The power of the Polish woman was wielded from the kitchen. It might take years of hard work trying to get them to accept me, and I could fail for I would never be other than an Irishwoman. Wrestling with imponderables, I had no guarantee of anything. On a good day, I felt I could take them all on; force them to accept me by keeping open house, throwing lavish parties, for no Pole could bear to miss a party. Adam would be proud of me, would settle down, and I would see to it that he never looked at another woman. On a bad day, I saw how it would be if I failed to grasp the language. People would be solicitous, speaking English for my benefit for a while, but would stop such accommodation eventually. I would feel ostracised, drinking more than was good for me to drown intolerable feelings of alienation, hiding behind a pretence of gaiety, acting the clown at the round of parties. On the outside looking in. Throwing my lot in with Adam could mean being marooned in a Polish ghetto. I might stop running in the woods, and Adam might stop singing or dancing the polka with his eyes closed.

Just as well my childbearing days were nearly over or I might have wanted his child. I could not imagine ever making shopping lists in my head with Adam, as I had with Stanley during the conjugal act. Was I not underestimating Adam? Surely he would want to protect me from all that, had had enough of Polish women now that his wife was dead. We could build a life outside the community, choose English friends. Apart from his connection with the church choir, he was a sophisticated cosmopolitan, at home in any company. Yet in my heart

Marie McGann

I knew it was only skin deep. He would miss the politics, the gaiety, the dancing, the music. I knew that unlike Ireland's freedom fighter Constance Gore-Booth, the Countess Markiewicz, I would have to go Polish. It could have been all right for her with no Polish community to contend with. And in any case, what hope was there of all that, when thoughts of Stanley haunted my waking hours and even my dreams?

Chapter Sixteen

THE LETTER

It seemed to me that life without the regular conviviality of social drinking such as I'd known in Ireland
was boring in the extreme. I knew I could have it
among the Poles. I had not found it elsewhere. Stanley
would not mix socially with the working class, and we
had tried and failed with the Irish University Club,
where he was seen as a West Brit with his gin and tonic
drinking and where I was bored by the wifely talk of
husband hunting by student domestic helpers, exorbi-
tant Catholic public school fees and the impossibility of
getting a decent meal in Ireland. I knew that if I could
pay the price, Adam would support me in the Polish
community, would not need to put me down to boost his
ego, for his ego was fine. Impeccably dressed, the Pole
exuded confidence and charm, regaling anyone who
would listen with tales of his prowess in many fields. I

understood it to be a compensatory mechanism for the temporary loss of his country. Who would keep his spirits up if he did not? He walked among the ladies like a cock among a scatter of hens.

So happy was I that Tom and Lydia were coming home that when I met Albert Uphill on the street outside my front door, he had little trouble inveigling me into the British Legion Club. He introduced me to the emphysemic doorman who stood up to greet the newcomer, and we went into a cheery atmosphere thick with smoke and the smell of beer. I said it was no wonder the doorman had emphysema, but Albert said he had got it in the trenches and the Legion always looked after its own. Bingo was on, so we sat in the darts corner and watched the rotund experts. Doctors and dentists would do well here, with the chain smoking, the mountainous tums, the disregard for the finer points of dental care, but psychiatrists and analysts would starve. The club was the front parlour, the home from home for the ex-combatant man of the street. He might get cancer from smoke but not from unhappiness. Permed ladies dressed to kill smiled knowingly at me, holding their cigarettes and their drinks at a refined angle, and I smiled back, delighted with such friendliness. You needn't leave the dog at home either. A big boxer puppy leaned comfortably against my leg and drank beer from a strategic mug under the table. Albert showed me photographs of his Burmese kittens. No Irishman would be capable of such an open display of sentimentality about animals. I found it endearing. After the third gin I blamed Stanley for snobbery. Hilda and Stanley would not have been seen dead among these friendly people. I had made an important discovery, and I kissed Arthur on both cheeks, which was probably a mistake. Loneliness and longing for conviviality need not drive me into the Polish community. Bingo and darts were easier to learn than the Polish language. I could always come back to the British Legion Club.

When I got home, I heard Fred's squeaky shrill barking, and he scampered into the garden with speed when I opened the door. He was beginning to transfer his lavatory from carpets to grass. I followed him outside. Inky black clouds obscured the church spire, but it was uplifting to think of Lydia and Tom coming home.

That evening I stood at my bedroom window, watching the darkness of night come charging over the distant hills, driving the daylight before it. A delicate rain dampened the pavements, closed the cherry tree blossoms for the night, and the moon heaved itself into the sky, silvering the tops of the roofs and the hills beyond. No honking call of wild geese in flight or lonesome cry of the curlew from the marsh here. No drunken din of the farmhands making their way home after a day threshing the corn and a night in the pub. Loneliness shrivelled my disinherited soul, and dropping the curtain I turned away. Sparkling water should be the drink of choice in the British Legion Club in future, or anywhere else for that matter. I should be looking forward to Lydia and Tom's return, not wallowing in a snakepit of alcoholic alienation. I need not become like others, isolating in baleful exclusion, flouting and flouted by the world. Misery was optional.

Stanley's letter came on the same day Tom and Lydia returned to claim the joyful Disraeli. They were in the back door smiling and were surrounded by the boys and Fred. We embraced. They thanked me for minding Disraeli for so long. Grandmother had died a peaceful death after her final stroke.

"Have you heard?" they both asked at once.

The letter was in my pocket.

"Yes, he's in Africa. I'll call you later. Thank God you're back."

I took out the letter after they had all gone to Tom and Lydia's house.

He was unable to travel to England due to circumstances outside his control and would be most grateful if I would come to Khartoum, where I would be met. A single return air ticket was enclosed. It had been posted from Wad Medani, a town one hundred miles south of Khartoum. I got a half-empty bottle of whiskey out of the suitcase at the back of my bedroom wardrobe, had nips of it with coffee, smoked, reread the lines trying to read between them. I telephoned the Polonia.

"Is this a bad time?" I asked.

"No time is bad for you. Delivery of champagne goes well without me."

"Stanley has sent me a ticket to go to Africa."

"Why does he not travel here?"

"Circumstances outside his control."

"How convenient. Only one ticket?"

"Yes."

"Your son is not to go then. How do you feel?"

"Flummoxed."

"Sorry?"

"Confused."

"Will you go?"

"I cannot think."

"Best not until I come. It may be better for you to go and finalise the situation."

Telling him calmed me. He would help me to do what was best. Best for whom though? He was hardly an objective bystander. I would not tell Malachy yet. Outside the windows white blossoms were turning pink on the hawthorn tree, and the deep red haws, left unscavenged by the birds, were darkening into purple. I pulled the grey hessian curtains over the festooned tie-back nets, mistakenly adopted from Hilda Uphill in an insecure moment to hide the faded fabrics of chair covers and the old Irish striped horseblanket rugs. I trained atmospheric floor lights on the Breughel's haymaking picture over the mantelpiece and Stanley's richly bound volumes of materia medica to highlight the sepia and crimson colours.

How could Stanley exclude the son he had not seen for over two years? It had better be a good reason after all this time, and I would have to travel to find out. Grim thoughts assailed me. Stanley could have found a way to get information to me if he chose. Neither war or prison could really stop Stanley Finucane doing what he wanted to do. All this was a trick to get me out there, and it was successful, for I knew that I would go. Curiosity and some kind of strange loyalty were operating, but the driving motivation was the need to try to straighten out my life. Could he be looking for a reconciliation? What will I do if he wants me back, Dad?

"Deal with that when it comes, Brigid Mary," John Rafferty's calm voice came to me.

I choose the green swirly dress and piled my hair on top of my head to look as if I were in charge of it all.

As I went to answer the doorbell, I heard Adam whistling cheerfully as he waited outside, and wondered resentfully what there was to be so cheerful about, but so smiling and elegant was he in a velvet mustard jacket and yellow cravat that I forgave him as we went into the sitting room.

"I can see you are deciding to go to Africa," he said.

"I believe I have no alternative."

"You have an alternative, but you are not looking at it."

"I am frightened for Malachy in case something happens to me."

"Nothing will happen to you."

"I have to consider every possibility."

"True. Yet you are not considering me."

"You can look after yourself, and Malachy can't. I think I will ask Tom and Lydia to be guardians. There is an insurance policy."

"I will take responsibility for Malachy if needs be. I will be father, for Stanley is no father."

"How could you be prepared to take on an adolescent child?"

"He is your son. He looks like you. He walks like you. And I have no son."

Dumbfounded I burst into a storm of tears, and he half carried me quickly and silently up the stairs into the bathroom, where we made love on the floor behind locked doors in case anyone came upon us. Every time was an adventure for us. A different journey. But fear of loss, of separation, of being caught in the act, with my head wedged between the lavatory and the bath, and his feet on the wall, drove us to a frenzy of new excitement and discovery in each other and, when it was over, to helpless smothered snorts of laughter. We nailbrushed the stains off his trouser knees and his new velvet jacket, which had fallen into filthy bath water left by Malachy. I would have done well to have addressed the bathroom mess rather than beautifying the sitting room, and I was grateful that Barowski's interest lay elsewhere than on the dirty bathroom floor. We managed to get down the stairs separately, tiptoeing silently like burglars. Barowski poured two brandies, and the thought of confining my drinking to sparkling water never crossed my mind. The alcohol ran through my body to my brain like fluid lightning, hopefully giving me the strength to tell Malachy.

"Stay with me while I tell Malachy."

"He sees me as an intruder. You must do it alone."

"Don't stay out of the room too long."

"Brid, you need to grow up. I will be in the garden."

I gulped the remainder of the brandy, went to the staircase and called Malachy down. Apprehension in his green eyes, he came into the room with Fred at his heels and a raised right eyebrow, which he had taken to practising in front of the mirror as an expression of his world view. I handed him the envelope, and he read the contents.

"From my father."

"Yes."

"Only one ticket. None for me?"

"We cannot make judgments, Malachy. We don't have information."

"What's stopping him sending information?"

"I don't know that either."

"We were doing all right without him. All this time without a word and now you are under orders to go to him and leave me behind. Are you going to go?"

"I married for better or worse."

"Gobshite, Mother. Hypocrisy is sickening in you."

"Don't speak to me like that."

"I don't know how else to speak. What are you doing with Pan Barowski then?"

"That is my business."

"Pardon me for breathing."

"Oh darling, let us not fight now. Can I call Pan Barowski?"

"Do whatever you like."

Malachy flung himself on to a chair as I rapped on the window. Barowski came in and, seeing Malachy hunched wretchedly near the doorway, took his hand and shook it gently. His presence diffused the pain-ridden tension between my son and me.

"My mother is going alone to Africa."

"Perhaps she has no choice," said Barowski.

"She can refuse to go."

"She can. But perhaps she needs to go."

"If I were you I would not let her go."

"If you were me you might be forced to let her go," said Barowski, crossing over to stand behind my chair.

"You are brave then."

"I am not so brave, Malachy. I am a gambler. You know I love your mother."

"Nobody told me you loved my mother. I don't know if you love my mother."

"You know now, because I tell you. I am not so stupid either. If I stop her, your father will stand between us always. He is standing between us now."

"You could have fooled me."

"It may not be obvious to you, but there it is."

Malachy's face crumbled, his lower lip stuck out and trembled. My heart laboured and I made to go to him, but Barowski clasped my shoulder from behind.

"Don't forget he is my dad and I miss him a lot sometimes. I want to go and see him with you, Mom."

"Oh darling, let me go first and find out. I promise you will see him again."

"Suppose you get hijacked?"

"Your mother has agreed that if anything should happen to her, and there is no reason why it should, I will take responsibility for you."

Malachy's face went slack and he stared dropjawed at Barowski. There was a long silence, broken only by the crack of sparks up the chimney and Fred's pompous snoring. Barowski held Malachy's gaze.

"I want my parents to be together with me."

"If that is to happen, I will not stand in the way. If that were to happen, there would be no point in contesting it."

Was he a man to throw in the towel like that? A man who would not fight for his corner or his woman. I was disappointed. I preferred the chimera of the artful, underhand gambler electrified by high stakes. It was left like that. Barowski and I went to the kitchen to make tea, and Malachy to his room.

The memory of the passionate encounter in the bathroom with Adam Barowski was to sustain me through a welter of conflicting feelings as I began to face the journey to Africa. How could Adam let me go, I'd wonder, and then console myself that he never expected me to reconcile with Stanley at all. Really he wasn't gambling at all. He believed he had the trump cards. Once a deserter, always a deserter, he would be thinking, and Stanley was again demonstrating his character defects in presuming that he could explain away the years of neglect and silence. There could be no hope of a reconciliation, for I was no pushover. When high, I would think that Adam was very clever, and when low, I would consider him to be Machiavellian, letting me undergo this hazardous journey to get what he wanted. He was letting me find out the hard way, for good.

I planned for the journey, suffering injections for small pox, hepatitis, cholera and typhoid. I began taking malaria tablets and took a list to the chemist in Boots, who read it and suggested I should go to Blackpool to see the lights instead. I left the list with him, sorry for him to be left behind in boring Boots, a feeling of excitement fluttering in my stomach.

I prised Zofia out of her house, if not her mourning, to go shopping. I would have to wear cotton from inside out to withstand the African sun, for silk was too expensive. Shorts were out. In a Muslim country the women were not expected to expose their heads, never mind legs. Since I always wanted more of everything, trying to fix my emotional insecurity from the outside, I would have recklessly over-spent except for Zofia, her erstwhile mettle beginning to show itself again. She had lived in North Africa and exasperatedly took control of the buying and spending. I acquiesced out of love. She made me put back skirts, saying I would be wearing a jellaba like everybody else. She drastically reduced the list at the pharmacy. Deodorant was a waste of money. Only God could stop you pouring sweat in Africa. So were sunburn cream, sunblock cream, wax hair conditioner. You kept your hat on or you went mad. Back went the water carrier, the candle for repelling flies, the camping knife with corkscrew and bottle top opener. It wasn't as if I were going to the jungle. Islamic society was very sophisticated, and surely Stanley would supply the necessities of life. We went to Harrods and had three gin and tonics in the bar. I said that I was in no position to know what Stanley would supply, and Zofia found kaftans, a safari hat, socks and boots. It was heart-warming to see the spring in Zofia's step, though admittedly helped by the gin, as we parted after the busy day. Zofia was a survivor and would live again, in spite of the Polish community.

I was surprised to find myself looking at spiritual books to take on the journey. Maybe I was afraid to die without researching the religious question. Fear swamped me without warning. Delia had said that all men are like the wild grass. The grass withers and dies, but the Word of God abides for ever. Delia so beloved and so long dead. Either the spirit of Delia was warning me or I had regressed to childhood out of fright. I bought the Bible, the Koran, the Bhagavad gita. There was nothing abnormal about being apprehensive before a long journey, but I would have done better to skip the gin the day before. Still, there would be a break from alcohol in Wad Medani, though Zofia said you could buy madly expensive whiskey and there was always *aragi* sold in the back streets.

I packed on the bedroom floor when Malachy was not around. I settled him and Fred with Tom and Lydia the day before I left to make it easier on us all. Adam came to see me on the last night. I was tearful, having said goodbye next door, and he was restless, eyes dark circled, following me around as I did last minute things. We didn't talk. What was there left to say? When I was finished and had booked the alarm call for the morning, he pulled me to him, holding my head against his chest.

"I'm leaving you now or I won't answer for my actions. You must try to sleep. Remember what we have is rare enough, and there should be a chance for us."

And then he was gone. I heard the front door bang behind him. He was gone without saying goodbye. Just like that. Just like that.

Chapter Seventeen

THE JOURNEY

I felt disembodied, travelling at a distance from myself, on the journey to Africa. It was disconcerting to watch myself leaving the house, dealing with the taxi driver, the luggage, clutching the bag with the passport, the traveller's cheques, the Koran and—bought at the last minute to study on the seven-hour flight—the children's guides to the Sudan and the Arabic language. While I was aware this phenomenon was stress-related and would pass if only I relaxed, I spent the journey to the airport observing myself, regretting and worrying. I watched myself staring blindly out at the traffic, reliving the last time with Adam, fretting because he had let me go, while knowing full well he could not have stopped me. I watched myself lose sight of the motivation for this journey, search for its justification, wish I'd brought my handbag flask, dry country or no dry country. What was

I doing? I was going to Africa to try to clear up the wreckage of the past, for my own sake and that of my son. I did not have any idea how this grandiose notion could be realised. No wonder I had abdicated to a safe distance from my body.

Arriving into Terminal 3 in Heathrow airport was like stepping on to an African shore, taking my mind off anxieties to such an extent that I felt myself inhabit my body again. There was one white person smelling strongly of whiskey among the crowd in the departure lounge for Khartoum. He introduced himself as an aeronautical engineer who was flying out to rectify disasters in Khartoum airport. It would have been wiser to have avoided Sudan Air, he said, which flew by the grace of Allah. I found his disparagement distasteful and vowed to avoid his ilk. Departure was delayed by two hours.

Flagging spirits were revived by the stunning smiles of the crew and the relief of getting aboard the plane, dry though it be. The combination of African and Arab blood had resulted in fine-boned pulchritude in these tall, thin Sudanese people, and I could see the temptation for the happiest of married men to acquire another wife or two. While I missed the finely engraved silver flask of vodka, my habitual companion in latter years (as if the elegant container took the harm out of the unladylike swig at my drug of choice), I knew that enforced abstinence from alcohol would be beneficial. It would help to keep my mind occupied with the children's books and the Koran on the flight. I had suffered too much emotional turmoil lately to be able to read anything about the country to which I now flew. Stanley had said the plane would be met. What the hell had he meant by that? What was I meant to understand from that, and why the hell had I not questioned it? Because my brain was becoming fuddled with drink maybe. If he intended to meet me, why had he not said so? Supposing he had meant that he was unable to come. What was the use of the journey at all if he was in prison, or sick, or too busy to welcome me? Was I mad to be on this flight?

Mad or not I was determined to hold on to my fantasy of flying on a magic carpet into the Arabian Nights. I opened the book on the Sudan. There were three geographical areas. In the north the Nubian desert stretched east to the Red Sea hills, and the Libyan desert merged with the Sahara in the west. The central zone, bisected by rivers and streams, was bordered by mountains in the west, and the Abyssinian plateau in the east. In the tropical south, where rain fell half the year, were the forests, swamps and savannah.

The Sudan, rich and fertile, was one tenth the size of Africa, and the stable foods were millet, groundnuts, sesame, dates, bananas, mango, guava, paw paw and onions. Vast areas of grazing land supported millions of cattle, sheep, goats, camels and donkeys. Acacia trees supplied most of the world's supply of gum arabic. The greatest tourist attraction was the wildlife in the 3,000 square miles of the Dinder National Game Park. Elephant, rhino, buffalo, lion, leopard, antelope and mountain sheep lived there. The variety of birds was unsurpassed. My excitement mounted as I read about the food, the animals and birds, and I was able to lie back in my seat, let my imagination wander from the

Nubian desert in the north to the tropical south of the vast country until I tired and slept a while.

The Koran, which I started reading when I awoke, claimed to be a literary masterpiece and one of the great books of prophetic literature. I also spent a few hours studying the Arabic-English book. The pronunciation was simple, and when I had read through it I joined the rest of the passengers in sleep, avoiding glancing out the window to be reminded of the altitude.

I was woken by the pilot's loud glottal-stopped singing to his darling, his Habeebidee. At least he was confident that Allah was holding up the plane. The floor was hot beneath my feet and condensation trickled down the window as we approached Khartoum. I dared to look out the window and was flooded with excitement to see the red baked earth and the royal palm trees of Africa under a great orange moon. The dawn broke as the plane circled over the city, and I was spellbound to see the sun, an orange furnace, edge into an indigo sky, turning the Nile into brass. I held my breath and braked with my feet as the plane descended and the pilot, still singing, taxied it along the runway. Whatever lay ahead, I would not regret the opportunity to walk on this exotic land.

Khartoum airport was an oven, packed with people. A fairytale oven. The heat drove the air from my lungs as we came into the noisy custom hall, crowded with tall smiling people. The men wore white robes, white turbans, the women brightly coloured flowing robes, with head-covering scarves. Delicately boned, chiselled-featured, many women had treble diagonal beauty scars on their cheeks, and the lower lips of the elders among them were covered in black tattooing venerating their age. Women squatted, feet flat on the ground, a posture I could not attempt.

I was glad to sit and wait for the luggage. It was as well I had not tried to smuggle in alcohol. The customs officials were giving the aeronautical engineer a hard time, ransacking his luggage. Apart from the giant electrical ceiling fans, there was no air conditioning, and clothes stuck to my body in a matter of minutes. Zofia was right. My shopping list would have been a waste of money. Sitting sweltering in my own sweat, I was too entranced with the people, too excited to be on African soil, to fret just then about Stanley. I was resolved to make the most of the journey, to live in the present moment like the great saints and stop fruitless analysing of the situation.

As we came into the arrival hall, clamorous with the incisively rattling Arabic greetings, I saw a card with my name and made my way to the bearer. A giant of a black man came forward smiling and bowed hand on heart.

"Salaam alaykum. Peace be upon you," he said.

"Alaykum salaam," I ventured.

Men did not touch women in greeting, yet vigorous slapping of shoulders went on among their own sex.

"My name is Dr Adil Asaker. I have come to take you to Dr Finucane," he said.

He picked up my luggage and gave it to the bearer of the placard, his driver. I went numb. My God. Stanley, the bastard, had not come to meet me. Stanley had not come to meet me.

161

Pride forbade me to ask where he was.

"Yallah. Let us go," he said taking my elbow.

"Shukran," I said stoutly, to cover my bitterness and shock.

I would not show weakness in this country, and especially before men. We went out through the throngs to a silver Mercedes car. The smiling driver, wearing his white crocheted hat at a comical angle over his eyebrow, opened doors and put away the luggage. The inside of the car was decked out like a sitting room, with curtains, vases of flowers and posters of well-endowed but covered-up lady filmstars.

"We have been dreaming of you coming for too many moons, Mrs Finucane," said Dr Asaker, smiling around from the front seat.

It was the first time that anybody had told me such a thing, and such warmth dissolved some of my disappointment and anger.

"You will need to recover from the delayed flight," he went on. Dr Asaker's smile nearly stretched the width of his face. I could see his magnificent back teeth when he turned around full face as the car progressed slowly in the jammed up streets. I learned that the people of Wad Medani considered Khartoum a necessary evil for commerce, but not a place to spend time in, unless forced to do so. The fearsomely sweltering streets were crowded with people on foot, on bicycles, on camels, in taxis, in cars French, German, English, even the odd Rolls Royce. There were queues for everything. Men stood in the blistering heat and women sailed to the top of the queue without waiting. I thought it was one recommendation for Islam and the Sharia law. I was glad to see the women turn it to their advantage at that level. I was proud to be one of them.

As we left the dusty white buildings behind, the driver rolled down a window and a welcome breeze came in. The land was arid, flat, with stunted trees. We passed villages of straw and mud huts, where children raced on donkeys, drove herds of humpbacked cattle, and men and women, graceful in their white and coloured robes, bent down to toil on the land. The penetrating heat was like a sauna, melting the aches and pains of the long journey. We passed a bus packed with smiling, waving people, some clinging to the roof and sides. There were glimpses of the White Nile on its way to join the Blue Nile at Khartoum, and after a time the vegetation grew luxurious, birds appeared in the scorching sky and in the trees.

Dr Asaker offered beer or iced water from a refrigerator under the dashboard, saying with a naughty grin that a good Muslim never drank before seven o'clock in the evening, but travellers were excused. A liberated man. I was grateful for the cold beer to slake thirst and give me Dutch courage to face whatever I had to face. Sooner than I expected we came to the pink courtyard walls, the tree-lined deserted streets of Wad Medani, looming out of the red dust.

"We are taking you to our home at our resting time, Mrs Finucane. This is the sixth largest town in our country. We numbered 630,000 at the last count."

The driver stopped at great iron gates and drove into a courtyard, where bougainvillea—crimson, purple, orange—covered the walls, the verandah, up to the iron corrugated roof. A heavily scented jasmine surrounded the teak double front doors, carved in stunning Islamic vegetal and geometric design.

"We have conquered the heat," said Dr Asaker.

Chapter Eighteen

THE HUSBAND

Dr Asaker had indeed conquered the heat. He led me into a palatial reception room, cool with giant ceiling fans, terrazzo tiles, and dark with shuttered windows. He guided me to a scroll-ended sofa covered in peach velvet.

"Dr Finucane is on duty until midnight. We have arranged for you to stay here for the present. It is more comfortable than the hospital where he lives. He works against our advice, you understand."

"I'm afraid I don't understand."

"He has not told you he contracted bilharzia?"

"He has not."

"He did not wish to worry you, I expect."

"I thought the least he might do was to meet me at the airport."

"I take the blame for that. I had a clinic in Khartoum

and insisted I collect you. The journey was out of the question for him."

"If he was well enough to work, I would have thought he could travel."

"Lives are at risk, the hospital understaffed. It was not an easy decision for him. It is not news to you that he is a stubborn man."

I felt small, mean-spirited. Yet here I was, and he had not even phoned to see if I had arrived safely. Dr Asaker was a mind reader.

"My driver telephoned the hospital as soon as you arrived."

"What is the nature of this bilharzia?"

"It's a drug resistant flat worm disease from the water snail."

"My God."

"The spores get into the liver through the sinuses and the hepatic portal vein. Stanley's lungs and liver are clear, but the intestine is not. The good news now is that he is responding to treatment."

"Do you mean he could have died?"

"Yes. We were afraid. We know now that he has the mansoni variety, which is not terminal, but other types are lethal."

Maybe he had sent for me to salve his conscience before he died. Maybe now that he'd had a lucky escape he would regret it.

"How did he get it?"

"He swam in infected water. The disease is endemic, and it is easily done."

My skin crawled squeamishly at such imprudence.

Could he not have stayed out of such filthy water?

"You must be relieved then," I said, trying to look pleased and relieved myself, though I felt only rising resentment.

"Very. It took a long time."

He rang a brass bell.

"You must sleep, but first meet my wife, Nahila."

A statuesque smiling woman entered carrying a drinks tray. There was no trace of subservience in the woman's queenly bearing. Placing the tray on a side table, Nahila bent down, placed hands on her husband's shoulders and then on mine, offering a cheek to be kissed.

"Welcome," she said.

Friendly black eyes and a generous smile were balm to my stressed spirit, and I smiled back as the doctor introduced us. I was to call them Adil and Nahila, and best to take a millet drink to settle me to sleep. Surprisingly the millet drink eased the craving at the back of my throat somewhat as alcohol did, and I drank a tall glassful before being shown to my room. As I fell asleep in the lace-covered bed under a whirring fan, I wondered if the journey were a waste of time. What was I going to discover that I might not have found out on paper? But I had wanted to find out for myself. I had to find out for myself, people said, when they forged ahead, wreaking havoc on themselves and everyone in their vicinity, despite all warnings and evidence as plain as a pikestaff of the inevitable devastation. I fell asleep.

Cacophonous bird call, frog croaking, dog barking, donkey braying and caterwauling pierced my sleep as the creatures of Wad Medani in live concert heralded the dawn of a new day. Jerked out of dreamless slumber, I lay shocked and disorientated by such an unaccustomed din. Irritably I switched on the reading lamp and looked at my watch. Five o'clock. No wonder the country was in trouble, with nobody getting a night's sleep. I jumped as a cock crowed in exultant gasconade just outside the window, where chinks of light filtered in through the blue wooden slatted shutters. Zofia had not thought of earplugs, but maybe cities were quieter than this small town on the White Nile. God alone knew what it was like in the south, with the roaring of the big cats, the rhinoceros or the elephant.

Exhausted, I slept again despite the noise and, awaking a few hours later, became conscious of a presence in the room. Stanley sat motionless in a chair beside the window. Except for the square set of the shoulders, the light grey eyes, the cleft chin, a different Stanley from the one I had last seen. The springy black hair was iron grey now, the face gaunt, dry-skinned, engraved from each side of the prominent nose to the pale long-lipped mouth. I saw that he was watching me out of the corner of his eye as I watched him. Flustered I pulled the sheet over my chest as he stood up, approached me, bent down and kissed my cheek.

"You were very tired," he said.

"How long have you been sitting there?" I asked.

"Not long. Fifteen minutes or so."

"You should have woken me."

"There was no need. You are as beautiful as ever."

"It's not so hard in this light."

"You always found it hard to accept a compliment.

168

Thank you for coming."

"It seemed I had little choice. I could not choose to leave my life and Malachy's life suspended any further."

"We will not quarrel now, Brid. Let me get you coffee."

"You sent no ticket for Malachy."

"I needed to see you alone first."

"And what about Malachy's needs? You never thought of them."

"I thought of them. I think of them. The decision to send one ticket was not made lightly, believe me, Brid."

He seemed taller than I remembered him as he left the room. Because of the weight loss, I supposed. He looked years older than when I had last seen him go to the clinic, not to return. I had had no insight then as to what was going on in his head. The plan to leave his family, his work in England, had been designed with care. He had been living in a dimension in his head I had been too obtuse to notice. Neither had I any idea what was going on in his head now. It was sickeningly humiliating to think that I might have never known what he thought or felt. I who prided myself on being psychic, the gift of the Celtic gods. Though just over two years since I had seen him last, it seemed in such a far-off time, in a far-off place. As if it had happened to a woman I could hardly recognise as myself. I felt again the weird situation of living at a distance from myself, watching the two of us now in a different world. Two different people in a different world, with cutlasses at the ready to be drawn and crossed, rattling sabres within minutes of meeting.

I got a robe from the suitcase, fled to the bathroom,

stripped off my sweaty nightgown and showered. Stanley was waiting when I got back with goat's cheese, freshly baked bread, a jug of coffee and an ashtray. I watched myself watching him pouring coffee and cutting up the cheese with careful deliberation. He had always been a man of deliberation in everything he did. I remembered his locating and opening a sunken vein for a blood transfusion, nearly twenty years before, when other doctors had failed. What manner of strange web were we weaving now, sitting around a table in Central Africa, he in his beautifully pressed white suit? Neither of us wanted to eat the cheese, and he lit cigarettes for us both as he had always done. It enraged me to see him cutting up the cheese with such cool deliberation, with the same nerve that gave him the right to walk out of my life and then into my bedroom without leave or licence. I felt the blood rush to my head and vowed to keep that head as best I could while on strange territory.

"We need to talk if you are up to it, Brid. How are you feeling?"

"The birds and animals woke me up."

"You'll get used to it. I'll get you earplugs for tonight. We will wait then until you recover."

"I would rather hear what you have to say, thank you."

"I wanted to go to London to save you the journey, but they would not let me travel. And I was badly needed here. The work is about life and death."

"How heroic. And more important than your own son. What I find difficult to understand is why you bothered to contact me at all. Why did you send for me?"

"I had come to believe that we owed it to one another."

"I owe you nothing. You wanted to salve your conscience in case you didn't recover from this self-inflicted disease. Could you not have been more careful?"

Stanley refilled the coffee cups.

"Being more careful, as you put it, would not have made much difference."

"Any difference might have made a lot of difference."

I had no idea what I meant, but I wanted the last word. In spite of my resolve to match his cool deliberation, I could not control my disappointment, my anger or the sarcasm in my voice, and longed for brandy to give me the courage to stand up to him. I had travelled too far to go out of control and give him the upper hand. He excused himself to go to the toilet, and I breathed deeply to calm myself and determined to let him lead the conversation when he came back. When he came back he was silent and we smoked without speaking. I would out wait him. He sat apparently relaxed, blowing perfectly formed smoke rings into the dust laden shafts of lights from the shutters.

After what seemed a long time he broke the silence.

"I asked you to come here because I had come to believe that we owed it to one another, and not to salve my conscience."

"You deserted us. You didn't even bother to write."

"Why did you come, Brid?"

"I need to get on with my life. To remind you that you are Malachy's father. Malnutrition and disease are not the only ways to destroy a child. Saving children's lives to

171

the detriment of your own son is criminal. What you did was criminal."

"I don't deny it. I want to make amends. I want to explain."

"How can you make amends to Malachy?"

"I can only try. In spite of what you may think, I knew very suddenly I had to go. I saw around me souls strangled with sophistication, shrivelled with cynicism, and my own soul the most moribund of all. I saw you failing to love me with any semblance of what I felt for you. I saw you engrossed with Malachy, and nothing in him of me or mine, only a challenging dislike of my company."

"Don't tell me you don't know that teenage boys rebel against their fathers."

"Try to have patience and let me finish, Brid. I had a depressive episode. I no longer believed in the work I was doing or our life together. I left my patient talking to herself about her hatred for her mother at thirty-five pounds an hour, went to the bank, to the hospital of tropical diseases, joined Unicef and flew to Khartoum to help halve child mortality by 1990."

"They must have been desperate to take you on such short notice. What gave you the right to abandon your son to the sick society you found so intolerable for yourself?"

"The compulsion to get out was overwhelming."

"I find that to be an excuse."

"I don't wish to excuse what I did. I want to tell you why I had to do it. I have rehearsed this many times."

"You have the advantage of me."

Stanley leaned across the table and took my hands in his.

"Oh Brid, I am sad to be the cause of such bitterness. I want to take that from you. I knew corrosive bitterness at what I had come to understand of our marriage, and I knew jealousy of Malachy, because he had succeeded where I had failed."

"Jealous of your own son?"

"It is common. I'm not proud of it, Brid. I'm ashamed of it."

"And what excuse have you thought up for not writing to us?"

"I don't expect to be excused. I am not offering an excuse. I didn't write at first because I was too confused to know what to say or how to say it. I guess I thought you both would be better off without me. Later I knew even less. Bilharzia can kill."

He released my hands, stood up and opened the shutters on to the African morning. Palm trees heavy with massive leaves and dangling clusters of flowers and fruit afforded some shade from the scorching sun. It all sounded so reasonable, so plausible, but then he had rehearsed this and was word perfect. Rigid with resentment I chose silence as my ally, watching with a heart of stone the familiarity with which he lit my cigarette with his own. He had avoided explaining how he had been taken on at such short notice by Unicef. I was suspicious that it had not been such short notice at all.

"I would rather not say what I have to say, but please hear me out."

"Say what you have to say,"

"It took me a long time to understand that you never loved me at all. You chose not to recover from your brother's death."

"What nonsense coming from you," I said, relinquishing the silence, handing him the power.

"It's safe to be in love with the dead. They cannot die twice. To risk love again was out of the question for you. You would not talk to the child psychologist your mother found for you."

"She needed one herself before she ever lost her son."

"You were a victim of a victim. Your mother was given to a spinster aunt to care for temporarily but never brought home again. Abandoned herself, she did the same to you, and compounded it by blocking you from your father as you grew. You turned to Shane. When he died, you withdrew from the emotional life."

"May I ask how you came by this information?"

"What I did not see for myself, your father told me before he died. He felt at fault for letting your mother demand all his time, his energy. He thought I might help you. I failed, of course."

Waves of desolation washed over me. John Rafferty looking out for me to the end.

"It's easy for the likes of you to call me a coward."

"I do not call you a coward."

"Have I travelled to Africa to listen to this? Why not tell me this before now?"

"John told me before he died, and by then you were not listening to me. I watched Malachy succeed where I had failed."

"Maybe you didn't bloody try hard enough."

"Correct. I should have forced you. Patience was the wrong approach. In the end it seemed futile. I gave up."

An undisciplined shoal of emotion flooded me. I felt as if he had blown a gaping hole in my stomach. Blown me to bits. I tried to stand up to leave the room, but my knees had dissolved and would not hold me up. Long shudders ran through the length of my body, and I could not hold back the tears. He knelt beside me and wiped my face with a table napkin.

"I loved you as best I could," I sobbed.

"It was not enough. In the end your repressed rage pushed you into clinical depression."

And I had thought him too insensitive, too preoccupied to notice.

"What am I doing here now?"

"I wanted to see you, to talk. For you to see where I live and work, and judge whether you and Malachy might join me."

"You must be crazy. Malachy wants to be proud of you. He thinks you are in jail, a political prisoner. He has tried to believe you needed to see me alone. Growing up is very painful for him. Can I send a cablegram to him today or telephone him?"

"You can do both from here. Adil will be glad to oblige you. It may sound crazy now, but maybe it's not so crazy. Oh Brid, I hate to see you cry."

He pulled my head on to his shoulder, and I wept without shame. He put me into the bed when I stopped and left me alone to rest. After he had gone I lay under a chilling vapour of sadness for the small child I had been. The little girl who ran from the room her mother entered. Thoughts crowded my head, buzzing like horse flies swarming around cow dung in the heat of the sun. I had thought that Stanley had been too busy, too insensitive to notice my depressive illness, and I had got it all wrong, it seemed. I resisted the notion that he had got it all right. There was no getting away from the fact that he had abandoned us, no matter how he rationalised it. Yet guilt raised an ugly head in my gut and refused to go away until I squashed it by blaming it all on Mary Rafferty and the God of my childhood, who when all was said and done had let such a dreadful thing happen to my brother, never mind His own Son. I managed to sleep as an innocent casualty of peace, clutching self-pity like a talisman to my victim heart.

Chapter Nineteen

WAD MEDANI

The sleep, whether of the just or unjust, did not last for long. Stanley's judgment was dangerously impaired if he expected me to sleep well after what he put me through. My sadness for the small child I had been became a hatred for the woman who never kissed her small daughter. Like a good Buddhist, I tried to dispassionately observe the powerful emotion swell and seep negative energy into the drumming heart and the furthermost crevices of my body, until a flaring remnant of self-righteousness faded. It worked eventually and I slept until woken by the strong musical call from the mosque some hours later.

I got up, showered and dressed in a white silk robe, bought in a fit of rebellion behind Zofia's back in Harrods. Zofia had said to put it back, that only rich and successful pilgrims to Mecca wore silk white robes, and

I'd better not give the wrong impression. I didn't care whether I gave the wrong impression or not, was glad to cover myself in its voluminous folds, so fragile and raw was I from Stanley's strong-arm tactics. Surely it was better to be blocked and locked than to stare at the horror of abandonment. I must ask Stanley to buy brandy to keep in my room.

A knock on the door was followed by a small boy who held his hand out, saying, "I am Saad. Come with me." He led me through a corridor bisecting the house to a courtyard, where Stanley welcomed me, settling me on a ground cushion beside a food-laden tablecloth. Nahila and Adil were prostrate on prayer mats under a shiny leaved eucalyptus tree. It was noon and time for prayer.

"Did you sleep, Brid?" Stanley looked me full in the face.

"Nothing to speak of, after our conversation," I said.

"I feel bad, flinging so much at you so soon."

"I feel bad for leaving Malachy behind."

Nahila and Adil joined us, dispersing some of the acerbity, Adil bowing hand on heart, Nahila smiling widely, henna-painted hands raised in greeting. Colonnades of palm trunks supporting palm branches made an effective shelter for the salads, stew, jugs of mango and guava juice. Nahila excused herself before we began to eat, and I was doubly disappointed at the prospect of segregation, as well as sobriety, even in this enlightened house. Knives and forks were laid but nobody used them. Bread was used to dip in the cobalt blue enamel bowls.

"Is it possible for me to send a cablegram home? To say I have arrived safely?" I asked.

"We will do it after you've eaten," smiled Adil.

"Adil has found a locum for me," said Stanley.

"By the grace of Allah. A dead hero is no hero," said Adil.

"The idle man rusts before the worker wears out," said Stanley.

"You are worn out," said Adil.

"I want to drive to Kassala, to show Brid the country-side," said Stanley.

"No colitis sufferer can undertake a 360 mile journey."

"The colitis is under control."

"Since when?"

"One week."

"It's not enough. The Land-Rover is heavy, the roads need tarmacking."

"That is not a problem for me. I drive in London," I said.

"If we share the driving, Brid, Adil will stop nagging."

"I may get a night's sleep if the driving is shared. Energy spent driving is lost to your healing, my friend. I will ask Allah to make safety your companion."

The man believed in God, and we got a blessing if not approval. Stanley, as always a law unto himself, sought approval from nobody.

Far better than a cablegram, Adil got me through to London and Malachy on the telephone.

"Malachy, it's me. Mom. I've arrived here safely."

"Where are you calling from, Mom?"

"I'm in Wad Medani, Malachy. Are you all right with Lydia and Tom?"

"I'm all right. When will you be home?"

"In a week, my love."

"Have you met my father?"

"Yes. Would you like to speak with him?"

There was a silence.

"Malachy?"

"I have to think about it."

My hands were shaking, my vision blurred with tears when I put the phone down. It had been so lovely to hear his voice.

Once the news got around the town on the White Nile of my arrival and Stanley's holiday from work, invitations came from people vying for the honour of offering us hospitality. The smiling people, the sights and the smells of the teeming town distracted my mind from the pain of separation from Malachy, from the confrontation with Stanley. It had not gone as I would have planned it. Instead of my confronting him about his desertion, he had cleverly confronted me with terrible things, turned it all around, shifting the blame to me and then saying it was not my fault either. It would have been different if Stanley had had to face Malachy, instead of attacking me. I should not have allowed him to dictate to me about our son. Forfeiting, as he had, all rights by abandoning us. Should I have brought Malachy? It did not make me feel any better when I saw how popular he was. I was a novelty as a visiting white woman, the wife of the hard-working doctor, and we would be invited for that reason alone, but there was general delight that he had survived bilharzia, and not only because it would be hard to replace him. There was more to it than that. I was shocked to find that he was loved. They did not see him for the deserter that he was. I saw it in their eyes.

Drinking lapsang souchong tea beside his swimming pool, I could not fail to see it in the merry marmalade-coloured eyes of Dr Omar Abu Bakr, and the blight of envy was bred in my despondency and uneasy self-esteem, twin legacies of the conversation the day before. Was it not dangerous for the doctor to announce loudly that any president who threatened to dump all the alcohol in the Nile was not fit to run the country, and that he had never trusted such a puffy faced religious politician jumped up from the army ranks? Neither of the men looked uneasy. They looked delighted to be together. Let them, I thought, and focused on the exotic surroundings.

The garden was ablaze with bougainvillea, and a baobab tree with its water-storing swollen trunk stood beside the flame-of-the-forest tree in scarlet flower all over the crowned dome. The early afternoon was filled with birdsong, and I was somewhat mollified that Stanley interrupted his discussion on the difficulties of educating the people about female circumcision now and again to distinguish the twittering of the weaver bird, the piping of the starling, the mewing cry of the yellow oriole for my benefit. I had not known he would be interested in the flora and fauna about him, but then it was beginning to look as if I had never known him at all. I could not make him out. The pallid man with unfurrowed brow and unruly iron grey hair, laughing and talking across the table, was a stranger to me. Let him be a stranger. I would enjoy Africa while I could, loving the heat, living in a sauna all day, toxins and tensions draining out of me. My mind might be in turmoil, but I was feeling no pain in my neck in the Sudan.

After affectionate goodbyes, of shoulder clasping and vigorous hand-shaking, Stanley managed to leave by promising to come back. I averted my eyes from the look on the man's face as we left, as if he had not expected Stanley to survive and did not want him out of his sight. And again I could not miss the naked love in the hooded black eyes of the genial octogenarian, Mr Bushy, as waving away his entourage, he joined us for lunch on the well-kept lawns of the Gezira Club.

"Peace of God," he said to me, with hand on heart.

We were served by white jacketed waiters, while thin cats scrambled for food and dogs sat quietly in the heat waiting for scraps. Mr Bushy wore a white silk jellaba, and I was grateful not to be wearing mine. In his day Mr Bushy had been minister for justice and was famous for throwing the British out of his country, even if they had built roads and schools and were less offensive than the French or the Italians. I thought wistfully of the homes for the elderly in England, as the old man's entourage of watchful bodyguards stood by in silent homage. Here the experience and wisdom of the old was held in high esteem. You could see how the people smiled and looked at him, as he got to his feet to go to a meeting. Stanley stood up, clasped the old warrior's shoulder with such reciprocal love in the watchful grey eyes that my throat tautened with jealousy. Why could he not have loved me and Malachy like that? But then had I ever looked at him like Mr Bushy did? I hid my pain behind a widely stretched smile.

"Look after him, my darling, and get him well," he said and walked erectly away.

I was relieved that we were seldom alone together in those early days, occupying separate rooms in Adil's house. I went to sleep with doors open on to the verandah, breathing in the Nile air, listening to the thin wild cry of the nighthawk. The custom of covering the head with a sheet while sleeping was suffocating for me, and I was grateful to Zofia for giving me a net veil to keep the flies off my face in the morning. I managed to distract myself from the unease of guilt and jealousy by the events presenting themselves daily. The brandy given me by Stanley was a nightly solace, measured out as carefully as I could to make it last, and I found that alcohol was served at many functions. At the Intercontinental Hotel the music played on a lyre—strings attached to symmetrically curved goat horns—and a goatskin drum kept stretched over burning charcoal, sounded so mellow that I determined, after a few gins, to bring back the lyre to England. Stanley encouraged me to drink a red leaf drink, excellent for urinary troubles. Having no such ailment I did not see why I should do as he told me. He was really warning me to go easy on the gin. If I had hoped for an enforced rest from alcohol, I had come to the wrong town. When all else failed there was *aragi* which, though tasting like diesel oil might, was swiftly and highly effective, and there was always the brandy in my bedroom at night.

Here in Wad Medani young heterosexual men strolled hand in hand in the streets, and old men walked straight backed, spitting with delicate precision on the ground. Young girls walked flirtatiously in groups on the crowded pavements, gazing at the luxuries of Arab life: filigreed silver, ivory or perfume in the shops. Unrepentant looking prostitutes kept an eye out for business on the street corners. African energy superseded Islamic decorum in some respects, and the yashmak was not worn here. Nigerian Ibos, a big-boned, smiling people fleeing from the Yorubas in their own country, and slender Ethiopian and Eritrarian refugees were absorbed into the life of the town. There were three million refugees in the country, mostly in the south. Stanley took me to the Nile to see the sunset. We found a seat made of logs and woven hemp under a canopy of mango trees, dark with roosting white-headed fish eagles, from where we could see the wide expanse of the river. Except for the frogs and the crickets, it was strangely quiet after the teeming streets. In the green sieved light, a weaver bird fed open-beaked babies in a woven nest hanging from a branch with a gossamer thread, and an orange-bellied parrot clucked at us from a high perch. We watched secretary birds stalk on long legs, a flock of pink flamingos launch into flight and the fiery sun slip slide down the technicolour sky, gilding the river as it sank into the horizon. Night enveloped us suddenly in inky darkness until the proximate moon, mottled with dark and light patches, shone its light and clusters of stars sparkled. Stanley broke the silence between us to point out the Southern Cross, the Plough, the brilliant constellation of Orion.

"Malachy is interested in the stars," I said.

"I will show him this one day."

"You never asked me how he was."

"I left you to tell me in your own time."

"He went into depression after your contact with us. He thought you were dead, that you had to be dead to abandon us."

He said nothing, and risking a sideways glance I saw his deep socketed face tense and ghostly white in the moonlight. What was the use of blaming a sick man? He had had his reasons, had explained his reasons, but it was easier for me to rubbish his reasons rather than look at my own truth. Demanding love and unable to give it. Screwed up by refusal to accept the untimely death of my brother, the only person to whom I had given unconditional love apart from Malachy. And where did Adam Barowski come into all this? Loneliness and sex confused the issue for me.

"Malachy came out of depression quickly. Joe gave him a healing."

"I'll write to thank him. Let me take you home. We have a journey to Kassalla ahead of us."

He held out a hand to help me to my feet, and I felt a current of energy flow between us. Perhaps it was the moon or a thought not to be entertained; perhaps I was any man's given the right circumstances, even a man who was afraid to talk about his son.

The next morning I experienced the morning din as an exhilarating live animal concert and the call to prayer a powerful reminder of the needs of the soul. I went with Stanley to see a small patient in an outlying village. Dogs and children surrounded the Land-Rover as we drew up in the cloud of red dust. The gate in the courtyard wall opened and the male relatives came out to greet us, to escort us inside, before we got out of it. The loving esteem and joy on the faces at the visit flummoxed me and, sitting surrounded by three generations of the family in the courtyard, I was unable to stop weeping for the dearth of such joy between this man and myself. No wonder he would not come back to England. No wonder he had left in the first place.

A fragile baby girl was placed in my arms with a sweet in the tiny fist in case she cried. Stanley took the sweet out of the baby's fist, opened my clenched fist and closed it in my hand. They rocked with laughter, and I got the message. I was not to cry now. I was to be happy for the baby was no longer in danger of blindness. The grandfather presented Stanley with a gold lighter for giving him back his granddaughter. The mother gave me a wooden carving of a woman's head, a photograph of the baby and sprayed us both with perfume. We refused food and drink. Goodbye to the men waving goodbye from the gateway, the women peeping behind, and the children swarming around the jeep. Goodbye to Mahomad, Macariam, Iptisore, and to all the children.

"In the name of God," said Stanley, the man I had written off as an arrogant atheist, long years ago.

Chapter Twenty

KASSALA

The bustle of activity around the Land-Rover in preparing for the journey to Kassala was exciting. The filling of the tank with petrol, the boot with spare cans of it, the checking of tyres, the packing of clothes, food, drink, first aid, and Stanley's medical kit were supervised with rapt attention by children and animals. Nobody actually wanted us to go. Saad and Montasir, his small brother, said it was "very danger".

We drove away at first light of morning, as the eagle owl shrieked farewell to the night and the parrots cackled a crazy greeting to the new day. Stanley intended to drive as far as possible in the cool of the morning, and I was to take over after we reached Gedaref some 200 miles away.

"We are heading for the Ethiopian border," said Stanley.

"I can see Addis Ababa on the map," I said.

"Maybe some day I will take you there."

"The Sudan is exciting enough for me."

"General Gordon saw it as a monotonous wasteland of tarantulas and fever."

"Is that how you see it?"

"Far from it. The Sudan could never be boring or unvaried for me, Brigid Mary."

I held my breath. He had never called me by that name since our wedding day.

We drove out of the town of Wad Medani through acacia and thorn-tree scrubland, where the houses of clay and mud had pyramidal roofs and foundations of stones to keep termites out of the walls. Hardy sheep and goats, thriving on scant fodder, were everywhere here, and flocks of noisy shrikes perched socially on the roadside bushes, until we passed into the silent interior, penetrated only occasionally by the spectral call of the hoopoe bird. I imagined I could feel the stirring of the soul of Africa in the silent scrubland.

Streaks of crimson light heralded the rising sun in the east as we reached the savannah plain where the nomadic Sukriya tribe lived in black goatskin tents set well back from the road. They bred racing camels. The savannah was an extensive grass-covered plain with no shade-giving trees, and we were glad to stop at the simple roadside refreshment places to drink black cinnamon tea with the Sukriya people. They looked to be a happy and hardy people, the faces weather-beaten but smiling, strong and purposeful. I was taken aback by Stanley's apparent mastery of the Arabic language, his ability to speak in the vernacular as he must be doing. Was it possible to learn such a complicated language in two years? A nasty suspicion that he had been preparing to leave me for a long time, secretly learning the language, even going to evening classes, entered my mind. If he had successfully hoodwinked me, then how could I trust him or anything he might say ever again?

Me and Stanley, Stanley and me. How easily it tripped off the tongue. Not so easy to wipe out all those years of knowing one another, or thinking I knew him, of having a child together—and foolish to try. Is that why I had come here? To try? As I watched with fascination the one-humped Arabian camels kneel down, whining and snarling through slitted nostrils, Disraeli's chubby chocolate face materialised in my head without warning.

"Disraeli thinks that most adults is lying pigs."

"He doesn't think it all the time."

"I didn't know camels were so bad tempered."

"They don't like being bitten by flies, and they are always irritable before the rainy season."

"When is the rainy season?"

"Soon now. They can smell it coming."

The camels were right. Battering plops of rain had become a torrential downpour by the time we reached Gedaref, a market centre for the surrounding savannah and the main trade route for the town of Gondar in Ethiopia. I sank to my knees in the mud and washed off at the bus station water pump, to the hearty amusement of the locals standing around. A woman baring her legs in public was unthinkable, but for all that the laughter was friendly. I waved and they waved back delightedly,

calling, "Kowajia, Kowajia." We sat in the jeep eating
chicken and mangoes outside a brick mosque with the
standard cylindrical minaret until the downpour lightened. Then we went inside. The prayer hall was bare
except for a thick-piled blue carpet. Light and shade
came from walls of intricately laid bricks and a blue
glass dome in the ceiling. Geometric designs in lapis
lazuli and gold covered the blue-washed walls. I was surprised to see Stanley kneel, touching ground with his
forehead before the wooden niche in the wall facing
Mecca. I could no longer think of him as an arrogant
atheist, for whatever he was—and I no longer knew who
he was—he was not either of those things. I knelt behind
the praying man. If I was a lost sheep, maybe I could be
found if I was willing to be found. My life was certainly
unmanageable. The gentle voice of my father rang in my
head.

"Remember your Creator in the days of your youth,
before the time of trouble comes, and the years draw
near when you will say you see no purpose in them."

I had done nothing of the sort, and perhaps it was too
late now. When Stanley got to his feet I followed suit,
asking him if he had joined the Islamic faith, but he did
not reply. I bridled, thinking he might as well have told
me to mind my business, but reminded myself he was a
sick man, and indeed he had always been a private man.
Far more private than I had imagined.

It was good to drive and let Stanley sleep, with the
rain a comforting drumming on the roof. Kassala was
on a straight run north, on the direct route to Port Sudan
on the Red Sea. I had to pull into the side for a herd of

camels occasionally, as they swung forward the right front and back legs first, and then the left front and back legs. The camel drivers smiled, hand on heart, calling, "Shukran Geziran," as I waited to let them pass.

Stanley looked peaceful as he slept. And handsome. Women had been jealous of me, quick to seek his company and loath to leave it. I had enjoyed their jealousy for it had heightened my triumph at carrying off such a prize. A young medic with a very bright future. I had not thought he would end up in the wilds of Africa. I had been a dog in the manger, not clear that I wanted him myself, but determined nobody else was going to have him. As I settled down to a steady fifty miles per hour, I wondered what Adam Barowski had got that Stanley had not got. Was there an embryonic companionship of sorts developing between Stanley and myself now that we had begun to talk from the heart, to give vent to feelings in a way we had never done? Too early to tell. I would have to tell him about Adam Barowski sooner or later. Whatever feelings I had for Stanley, contempt was no longer paramount. It was hard to look at the part I had played in it all, projecting my own stunted growth and cowardice on to him. Whatever he was, he was not the coward I had made him out to be. That thought was too painful to hold, and I welcomed another, rising like a genie: that when all was said and done he had buggered off and left Malachy and myself without a word for two years.

The rain stopped as suddenly as it had begun, and Stanley woke up insisting on taking the wheel. We left the flat plains of the savannah behind and drove into the

hilly country of the Kassala province, which incorpo-
rated the last of the Nubian desert in the north. On our
right shone the lake Khashan El Girba, fed by the Atbara
river flowing from the heights of Ethiopia, and further
on the Fou and the Taka mountains shimmering purple
in the searing sun. The sight of the remote high-walled
town, surrounded by mountains and desert, with eagles,
vultures and buzzards wheeling above, was for me the
epitome of romance, lifted out of the Arabian Nights to
be the highlight of my visit to Africa.

We drove through the teeming streets and drew up at
the Lake Toteel Hotel. There was, wonder of wonders, a
bar and a clean bedroom with two single beds. Stanley
had his two brandies and I my three gin and tonics as we
waited for the kebab meal of spiced lamb, unleavened
bread and steamed bananas. Afterwards, when the heat
of the day was over, we went out. I wore my white robe
and Stanley a sleeveless twill shooting jacket and khaki
shorts, showing the hairy muscular legs I had forgotten
about. The bulk of the population was out, the shops and
cafes throbbing with people. Taxis blaring horns nudged
supercilious camels on the wide thoroughfare lined with
palm trees. A booth of smithcraft stood next door to a
shop selling camel saddles of yellow wood and red dyed
hide. There were short daggers in leather and snakeskin
scabbards, with a loop to go around the upper arm,
which I thought to buy for Malachy, but Stanley said they
were too dangerous for a teenager. Less dangerous than
an abandoning father, I thought.

I focused on the marvellous slabs of cotton, for cotton
was king in the Sudan, and the displays of jewel-

coloured woven carpets. We sat in a crowded cafe among old men sitting around knee-high clay gourds, smoking *happi puppi* through long brass pipes and clicking fingers in time to radio music. I was nervous to be surrounded by fierce looking frizzy haired tribesmen, the Hadenduah. Stanley said they would not touch anyone unless they felt insulted by them. The Brits had called them the Fuzzy Wuzzies. They carried big swords which they made themselves and came down from the Red Mountains to buy horses. I worried that they looked so serious and unsmiling, but Stanley said they were busy looking at a white woman, and I should smile first. I did, and was rewarded by sunburst smiles. The women wore collars of bark interwoven with coloured beads and skirts of dyed goatskin. After a while the men lost interest and wandered off, the women trailing behind them.

I was glad to get back to the lantern lit garden restaurant in the hotel grounds, where Stanley ordered drinks, lit cigarettes as we sat under a lone tamarind tree in purple flower. The tamarind tree was too acidic for other trees and always grew alone, Stanley said. Singers ate the green leaves to improve their voices. What a fund of knowledge he had about his new country already.

"What was wrong with the little girl in Digdir?" I asked, curbing my bitterness.

"Trachoma. Endemic conjunctivitis. The inner surface of the eyelid is inflamed, granulated. It can blind for life," Stanley said.

"No wonder they think you are God."

"Can you imagine the pain?"

I was ashamed of my inference that he worked for

self-aggrandisement and asked for a gin and tonic. We were silent in the fragrance of the yellow hibiscus and oleander bushes. A bat hung upside down on a branch, the only power-driven flying mammal in the world, according to the stranger sitting opposite to me. He said it looked like a flying fox specimen and I said it looked like the devil. An eagle owl blinked hugely through ping pong eyes at me.

"What are you thinking?" he asked after a while.

"That you will never work in England again."

"Preventive medicine is the weak link here. I am committed. Are you glad you came, Brid?"

"Yes. It's a new world."

"Africa steals the heart and then the soul."

"I see that."

"Are you glad you came to see me?"

"I am glad you believe in what you are doing."

"That is not what I asked."

"I am glad to be with you. I wish you weren't sick."

"My sickness will pass."

"I have met a man in London."

"I saw there was something new about you."

"He wants to marry me, to take on Malachy."

"What does Malachy say."

"He likes Adam Barowski. He is angry with you."

"What do you want, Brid?"

"I cannot see ahead."

"He must be very sure of you to let you come here. A gambler for high stakes. Can you live in a Polish community? It might be an unhealthy situation for you."

"Perhaps no situation is healthy for me."

"Oh, Brid."

"It's too late for you and me now."

"It is not too late. You have changed. You are more open, more vulnerable, and should be careful what you do with the rest of your life. You know me. We have spent half our lives together, have a son together. You could come here. I am very lonely sometimes."

"And Malachy."

"There are choices. He could finish his education there or in the Sudan. We have a new university in Wad Medani."

"You are facing me with impossible alternatives."

"Take the time you need. Everybody speaks English in Wad Medani, and if your future career is a consideration, we can guarantee you a lectureship at the university."

He had certainly thought of everything. We had a supper of veal, tomatoes, rice and a bottle of red wine, and went upstairs and to sleep in separate beds. Before I lost consciousness, the thought crossed my mind that I could have slept with Stanley, and it was far from unpleasant. So much for fidelity to Adam Barowski. In the morning I was glad it had not transpired, for I was not ready to walk away from the Pole.

Chapter Twenty-One

CONFRONTATION

I was afraid I wouldn't be ready to leave Stanley either. I said farewell to the Asaker family, and Adil came out with me to the front of the house where Stanley was testing the Land-Rover's engine.

"Will you come back?" he asked.

"I don't know," I said.

"We don't want him to leave the hospital. It took us long enough to get him to take the appointment."

"What do you mean?"

"It's nearly ten years ago since he first approached us, but could not make his mind up. Come back," he said and kissed me.

What a shattering disclosure. My suspicions were spot on. Ten years. Ten years planning to go. All nonsense about his breakdown being the cause of his departure. More fool me to have taken all the blame and listened to his excuses for abandoning Malachy. I hid the feelings of contempt and betrayal as I accepted the copper gourd of brandy he gave me for the journey. If I were careful, he said, I could have the odd nip in the toilet without the crew noticing. As the time came for departure the thought then that we might never see one another again left me icy cold.

"Oh Brid, come back," he said as he kissed me. "Please come back with Malachy. I love you both."

Fine sentiments, I thought sarcastically, as I looked back and waved from the departure lounge door, but he looked so wretched and lost, as I'd never seen him before, that I felt an overwhelming compassion for him and then guilt. Did he not have a case after all? Could any man be happy with a desolate-hearted woman?

"I may come back with Malachy one day," I called to him from the departure door, feeling as wretched and lost as he was.

I followed the passengers for London on to the plane, walked past the crew into the lavatory to kill the pain with the brandy. I sat on the lavatory seat, gulped it down and felt better. After all, I would be under an obligation to accompany Malachy when he visited his father in Wad Medani. Not even Adam Barowski could expect me to allow a teenage boy to take that journey alone. Oh yes, there was no doubt that I would see Africa again. Where the birds flashed crimson and gold along the Nile banks by day and the flying foxes hung upside down at night. Where else could I listen to the shriek of the nighthawk and read Sufi poetry by the light of the moon? Nobody could stop me coming back to my

Africa of the lute and night-long dancing to the beat of the goatskin drum.

I sprayed my mouth with breath freshener and walked with careful dignity to my seat. Strapped in, I looked out the window at the banked-up clouds through a gathering mist of alcoholic tears. Oh yes, I would go back to Wad Medani, where the people smiled from the heart and young men walked hand in hand on the streets. Where the poorest of the poor shared bread and children suffered from malnutrition but not from emotional abuse. Back to Africa, to hear the sound of the flying beetle ricocheting off the window shutters, and to drink *aragi* under the star-white sky. I had many more nips of brandy during the journey without attracting attention, until the copper gourd was empty and I without a care in the world.

When the plane landed in London, my lungs, accustomed to the clean Nile air, mutinied and I gasped in the taxi home. The sky was nearly as dark as a sand-filled sky, and it seemed to me that the only difference between the lethal atmosphere in the airport and in an African sirocco was the advice not to move in the latter. Gazing out the window at the London traffic, I wondered if I would become the sort of woman my mother warned me to stay away from, a woman without moral fibre who would leave her husband for another man. I thought of the English girls who had been in and then out of my life who had done just that. Highly sexed lovers of life and fun, carrying their baggage with effrontery from one lover's bed to the next lover's bed. Lost children suffering from drunkenness, abortions and the dissolution of love. I was not like Trilby who left hers for the soulful eyes of a petty thief, with her two failed suicide attempts, unlike her sister who succeeded the first time when her dog died of old age. Nor was I like Diane who gave her all to men at the drop of a hat, now living in wealth with a husband and an afghan hound and threatening to do it all over again. Such pain and loneliness behind the wild gaiety. I was not like them. My husband had left me. Denial, justification and blame. The thinking of the alcoholic, though I did not know that then.

I had never looked at another man or neglected my wifely duties. Hadn't I gone to cordon bleu cookery classes, entertained his colleagues? Yet Stanley maintained I had driven him away. I shivered, felt ill. Sourly I thought I could have expected more of Stanley than to buy cheap brandy, but then had he not often been parsimonious with his money? I could not remember. The house was in darkness. I felt too ill to go next door to Malachy, and I climbed the stairs without putting on the lights. I locked myself in Malachy's strangely tidy room, clutched his old teddy bear and dreamed of Mary Rafferty flying across the African moon on a pink flamingo.

"Show me your company, and I'll tell you who you are," she said.

"I'm not like them," I replied.

"You could not keep your man."

"I never tried to keep him."

"Every woman worth her salt knows how to keep her husband."

"My dad was a saint to stay with you," I thought in my dream.

I knew better than to say it even in my sleeping state.

"Get down on your knees and thank God for a second chance," she said.

"Ah shit," I did say aloud.

The formidable Mary Rafferty was speechless.

Loud sounds like the bellowing of bull frogs or the thundering gallop of camels across the savannah plain woke me to Fred's excited barking, to Lydia and Tom calling, to Malachy and Disraeli galloping up the stairs. There was Fred licking my face, hugs and kisses from the boys and Lydia and Tom. All talking and laughing together. It was worth going away to get such a welcome back. What had I brought from the Sudan? Lots. Woven string bags from the Angasanah Heights, indigo blue cottons worn by the famous desert Tuaregs, scarlet plumed army helmets, made famous in the Victory Day Parade in London. It would all have to wait until after school, after work. They tore themselves away, departing noisily, leaving Fred draped across my lap.

I was glad to be alone when Adam telephoned. Would I be rested enough to receive him that evening? It seemed such an age since he had last seen me. Was everything settled? More or less, I lied. What did that mean? I did not know what it meant, so I sidestepped it, said we would talk later, and that I would look forward to meeting him, which was another lie, for I was suddenly afraid to meet him at all. But because I had never done things by half, I invited him to dinner.

I had time to unpack, to shop, prepare food, have a drink of vodka from the suitcase in my bedroom, reluctantly wash out the smell of Wad Medani and the vodka before Malachy arrived in the back door from school. I had stopped using peppermints to kill the smell. It made people suspicious.

"Tell me all about Africa and Daddy, Mom," he said throwing his satchel on the floor.

"It'll take weeks to tell you all, Mal. Daddy was sick, but is wonderfully recovered. He is doing marvellous work saving children's lives. You can be very proud of your dad."

"Was he too sick to contact us?"

"He was, Malachy. He didn't know if he would live or die. He wants you to go there."

"When will I go? Will you come with me? Did you see the Hadenduah?

"I saw the Hadenduah. You may go after the exams, but I don't know about me yet. Africa is wonderful, Malachy. Your presents are upstairs."

Malachy hugged me, kissed me twice and raced up the stairs. Teenagers were unpredictable. I was glad he hadn't asked if Stanley and I were getting together. That would come later, I supposed. I must try to protect him from my own confusion. Once you had a child you could never again behave as if you had not.

I looked up Polish dishes in my seldom-opened cookbook, thought of Stanley warning me to be careful of my life and found myself sipping red wine, peeling beetroot for *barszcz* soup and stuffing cabbage leaves with mince meat and rice for *galumki*. A Polish meal for a Polish suitor. Parting from Stanley at the end had been unexpectedly hard, and I had told him I'd be back. Back to the smiling Asaker family, to the proximate moon and the falling stars in the night sky. Look at what the Polish community had done to Zofia because of her failure to conform. Had Adam given due thought to the consequences of bringing a Gael into that society, of what the women would do to him, never mind to me. Life in Wad Medani with Stanley could be a joyride in comparison with that.

On the other hand I could join the Franciscan secular order as a celibate Christian and avoid losing either Stanley or Adam. Neither of them could fault me for leading a holy life. I was heartened by the wine and this novel idea of life devoted to Christ, going about in a long brown habit with a begging bowl.

It was early evening when I came downstairs in my swirly green dress, but the sun still shone like a flame through the orange flowers and the delicate green fronds of the plants on the windowsill. A strong fragrance of roses came in through the open window. I watered the plants kept alive by Lydia in my absence and lit a fire for comfort. Engrossed, I didn't hear Adam's knock at the front door or his entry through the kitchen at the back.

"Welcome back, Miss Finucane. You are a sight for sore eyes."

I dropped the poker. Had nobody taught him to knock before entry? Immaculate as always, he wore a navy suit, striped in pink, I'd not seen before. I was unprepared for the magnetism, the fine dark eyes, the mobile mouth, but I stood my ground on shaky legs as he bowed and kissed my hand. He evidently felt free to walk through my house as if it were his own. Could he be staking his territorial claim already? He would find that I had something to say about that. I offered to make martinis and brought them to the fireside chairs. We sat opposite to one another.

"It is very good to have you home, Miss Finucane," raising his glass.

"I am not called Miss Finucane."

"Pardon me, Brid. I guess I liked to emphasise your single state. You have not caught the sun."

"No sunbathing allowed in 105 degrees."

His smile did not reach his half-lidded eyes.

"You say that things are more or less settled?"

"Your eyebrows don't meet in the middle," I said.

"I can make them meet in the middle," he said.

"It's not the same, making them," I said wildly.

"How unfortunate. May I know the significance of middle meeting eyebrows?"

"They're a sign of high intelligence and bad temper."

"Better as they are then, don't you agree?"

"You asked me if things were settled, and I said more or less instead of less rather than more."

"May I know what you are saying then at this moment?"

"Stanley is recovering from a serious illness. He wants Malachy and me to go there to live. He works with Unicef."

"He must be crazy."

"He will not work in England again. His work is life saving."

"Are you telling me his illness prevented him contacting you regarding his whereabouts for two years? Do you mind if I smoke?"

"The dinner is ready."

"I am not impressed by Dr Finucane's altruism."

Adam walked across the room and looked out the window at the close of the summer's day. The clamour of swallows playing tig over the chimney pots and the sonorous ticking of the clock in the hall filled the silence.

"Divorce him and marry me," he said, turning around.

"I cannot see my way forward just now."

"He walked out on you and your son."

"I am only beginning to understand why he had to do it."

"Dog's blood, but you have the advantage of me."

He looked as cold and as dangerous as a glacier in a high mountain pass.

"Am I to understand that you brought me here to tell me that you intend to join him?"

"He said I wouldn't survive in a Polish community."

"What the hell does he know about the Polish community?"

"There is some truth in it."

"What bloody truth, excuse my language?"

"I'd have to learn the language."

"So, learn the language, don't learn the language. You have always understood my language, Madame."

"I am asking you to understand mine. I tell you I am confused, tired and frightened, but you're too angry to hear me. I understand your anger, and I take responsibility for it. I had no moral right to be your lover."

I had gone too far, had said too much, and the conversation was out of control. His face lost colour; the shadows under his eyes were a dark bruise.

"Correct me if I am wrong. Are you saying our relationship was immoral?"

He had used the past tense. I felt the beginning of a severe headache.

"I'm saying I had no right to it. No clear way to make a commitment."

"You dismiss love and hide behind archaic church rules, when the truth is you are too cowardly to love anyone. I am beginning to understand your husband's departure."

I was making a terrible mess and would fall between two stools and be alone for what was left of my life.

"He wants to reconcile with me and Malachy."

"Are you blind? Can you not see that no decent man would do what he has done? His behaviour was that of a scoundrel. Only a scoundrel would leave his wife and child without contact for two years."

"He was sick. He is sick." I heard myself defending Stanley.

"Christ Almighty, I would not have thought you to be such a fool. In any case, you cannot give him what you have not got."

"I ruined his life, and I blamed him for ruining mine."

"He is putting his life to good use now. You could leave him alone."

"He doesn't want me to leave him alone."

"That suits you. For you, love is too dangerous."

"Maybe I don't know what it is any more."

"Love is what people query when they don't have it. It hurts, and you, Madame, are a coward."

"I can't help it."

"You can help it, and nobody can do it for you. I was trying, but no more. Do not bother me until you know where you are going, as I shall not bother you."

Monumentally angry, he left the room without kissing my hand, without tasting the meal prepared with such concentration. I heard him bang the front door behind him. He was gone. Just like that.

Chapter Twenty-Two

THE DRINK

I heard him start the engine and drive away. He really was gone then. He did have the audacity to walk out on me and the Polish dinner I had gone to the trouble of preparing for him. Numb with shock, I turned off the gas under the bubbling borscht soup and slowly climbed the stairs to my bedroom. I found it difficult to understand how the evening had ended in such a manner. How a sophisticated man like Adam could be so lacking in tolerance and understanding of my mental confusion, my fatigue. Maybe it was as well to find out these things in time. The only people who had ever understood me were gone from me long ago. Tears of disappointment, of self-pity, scalded the pit of my throat. He had the audacity to accuse me of deep-seated cowardice, of a pusillanimous need to live in safe waters, when there were no safe waters anywhere and my life was like walking on thin-crusted lava. Any sane person would advise me not to move until the lava cooled into rock. What was so wrong with prudence as to enrage him, to turn him into a wild ass of a man like Ishmael in Genesis? Any rational man would have known better.

It was a comfort to blame the evening's debacle on his irrationality, to block the thought that his disappointment was natural. So that was that. He had not been rational, and all I had to do was to give him time to come to his senses. We both needed time to analyse the situation with all its ramifications and to reach a well-thought-out decision, for neither of us was in the first flush of youth, and it was foolhardy to behave as if we were. I would say as much when he rang in the morning. Sleep on it, people said, when appropriate action was unclear. We would have time to sleep on it, before he rang in the morning.

Only to my consternation, he did not ring in the morning. I couldn't believe it. The phone must be out of order, but the exchange said it was not. He must be frantically busy in the Polonia, but there was no call that evening either. Or the next day. Or the next. Did he intend to keep this game up, sulking like a baby who's thrown the rattle out of the cot? If he was trying to punish me, to force me to call him, he would find out that I was not to be manipulated into submission. No man was going to tame me like that. My mother had said you must start as you mean to go on with men, and for once I agreed with her. He would never be able to maintain this silence, to keep this up. He did keep it up.

False expectations were a double bind. Disappointment and the humiliation of wrong judgment. I tried to comfort myself with red wine but found only a progression to bitterness which drove me to open a bottle of whiskey, for wine was not strong enough to dull the chagrin. I was back nearly two weeks from Africa when Father Joe came in the back door unannounced. So consumed with hurt pride was I, and so ashamed that the second man had left me, that I had found excuses to block him since I had come back. He had come in silently, spring-footed in trainers, and I watched his face change as he saw the half empty glass and the whiskey bottle.

"Out with it, Brid."

"Stanley wants me back, and Adam has walked out in fury."

"He won't go far. Is Stanley staying in Africa?"

"Yes."

"Well, he is not going anyplace either. What do you want, Brid?"

"I don't know."

"Alcohol won't solve it for you. Are you drinking daily?"

"Round the clock more like."

"Can you lay off it for a while?"

"I don't want to."

"It magnifies loneliness. Nobody knows that better than us priests. Is Malachy gone to camp yet?"

"Malachy goes next week."

"He must know about your drinking."

"I hide it from him. I keep it upstairs in a suitcase."

"Kids don't miss much. I'll call you with the number of Sobriety."

"What is that?"

"The experts on how to stop drinking, and stay stopped."

"I'm not an alcoholic."

"I did not say you were. Don't drink any more now. Let me call Zofia."

"I'll call her myself if I need her."

"It would be good if she could go with you. In the meantime, God go with you."

"Where is God?" I shouted after him, but he was gone into the garden.

I did not do as he asked. Obedience was not a strong point with me, and defiance always had been. How could I be expected to sleep without a strong nightcap? I poured myself a whiskey and soda and was far from sober when Joe rang with the number of those people. The feelings of humiliation and disappointment drove me to turn the radios on all over the house. I was careful to hide the bottle, to wash out my mouth with mint disinfectant, before letting Zofia or Lydia or any other callers in during school hours. I would pretend to be busy, talking non-stop in a breezy manner to forestall questions. I even took to putting on an overcoat when the doorbell rang, as if I were about to go out. If they were not fooled I did not want to know about it, and in any case nobody stayed very long. I saw to that. I was glad for Zofia that Anja was back at home, that they were getting on despite Anja's decision to have the baby, but I was also glad that she didn't stay long. I was not ready to tell her about my state. I managed somehow to get Malachy off to summer camp, the sadness I felt at seeing my thin young son stride gallantly across the street and into the coach tinged with relief that I could now drink in comfort.

The fact that I was grateful for Malachy's absence should have alerted me that something was very wrong, but it did not. It took waking up naked on the bedroom floor beside a smouldering mattress and an empty bottle of whiskey, the purpose of my life extinct, to do that. I came out of that blackout with what I was to learn were the Four Horsemen of the Apocalypse—terror, bewilderment, frustration, despair. These feelings drove me to telephone Sobriety, the self-help group for alcoholics. A plummy voice wanted to know if I had drunk that morning and when I said no, asked if I could get to the meeting near by in the church hall. Did he think I was a last gasper? I would see if I could find the time. He suggested I make it a priority, gave me the address, took my address and would send me the literature. The call did my hurt pride no good whatsoever, and I was in mind to complain about the high-handed people manning the telephone, but thought they were in any case a pack of ex-drunks, of social misfits, while I was just going through a hard time, for which I blamed Adam Barowski, Mary Rafferty and God.

The morning post brought a list of meetings and a questionnaire. Whatever faults they had, tardiness was not among them. The questionnaire had fifteen questions. Did they think people had nothing better to do than spend all that time on such a list? I sat in my string-bottomed chair, cigarettes and whiskey beside me, and began. Saying yes to one meant that one was in danger, to two meant that one was in all probability an alcoholic. Glancing down the page, I thought I might very well say yes to them all. Any law abiding citizen might say yes to them all. I went down the list deciding for yes or no.

Number one. Did I vary the places I purchased alcohol to hide the amount I did buy? Of course I did. Prying neighbours would relish blaming my drinking for driving the poor hard-working doctor away.

Number two. Did I hide the empties and dispose of them secretly? Naturally I did. What was to be gained by broadcasting my private affairs to the dustmen. I preferred to put the empties in the car and take them to the rubbish dump after dark.

Number three asked if I rewarded myself with a drinking bout after working especially hard. It was human nature to like a reward for hard work, and if I was not good to myself, then who would be?

Number four. Was I often permissive to children out of guilt for alcoholic behaviour. I lit myself a cigarette, drank whiskey and chuckled over that one, because I had always been permissive with Malachy, drink or no drink. A fabulous mother, even if I said so myself.

Number five sobered my frivolous mood, for I did have the odd blackout about which I could not remember a thing. Worrying that really, and a sign of advancing old age. I was indecisive about number six, for while I had not had to ring up a hostess to apologise for behaving badly, I might have done so if I'd been to any party.

The thought of having joined the ranks of drink-sodden, clothes-shedding ladies, from whom I had long averted my contemptuous gaze, was not to be borne. Neither could I consider how I might appear to a fly on the ceiling, never mind God, after an evening's drinking in my own sitting room, where Malachy might wake up and come down at any moment. I sipped the whiskey and soda and lit a new cigarette. There was no point in abandoning the questionnaire now, and besides it was fun of a sort.

Number seven. Stanley and I always had a few drinks to get in the right mood before a party. Everybody did. It was a simple precaution in case drinks were delayed or frugally served, as in some houses where a half glass of good wine was expected to last. Such establishments got struck off the visiting list.

Number eight. Did I feel wittier, more charming when drinking? I would write a strong letter to Sobriety for composing this silly questionnaire. Everyone was wittier and more charming when relaxed, and impossible to be either when clearing up Fred's dung or addressing the kitchen sink. What else did one drink for, for God's sake?

Number nine. Did I feel panicky in facing alcohol-free days, as in visiting relatives? How insular. The bottle would be on the table in a flash in Ireland or on the Continent. Even grandmother Delia had been partial to a drop of whiskey. Setting aside the cultural assumption of dreadful Sunday visits to in-laws, balancing tea cups on laps in the front parlour with flying ducks on the wall, I wondered how I would feel about making tomorrow a dry day? Never mind which tomorrow. I put a cross on that one to be answered later.

I answered no to number ten, which asked if I invented social occasions to drink, for I didn't need social occasions to drink.

Number eleven was no also, for I did not avoid television on alcoholism when others were present and bone up on it later. Far from me was the television addict with the bottle hidden in the aspidistra plant behind the lace curtains.

I said yes to number twelve, as I had carried drink in my handbag for many years. In fact I never went out without it these days.

I said yes to number thirteen, for I certainly would become defensive if anyone had the audacity to mention my drinking.

I said yes to fourteen, for of course I drank under pressure or after an argument, like everyone else.

And I had to say yes to the final question, number fifteen, for I had driven after drinks and felt in control. And I had been in control and sod anyone who said different. I poured a finger of whiskey and sipped it to celebrate the end of the silly questionnaire.

Unsteadily I counted the yeses. Twelve yeses and a maybe. Damning evidence according to them. But then who were they? It was me against them. Giggling I went up to bed, and knew no more that night. Next morning I looked at the burnt mattress once more, and again faced the day with the Four Horsemen of the Apocalypse.

Chapter Twenty-Three

THE MAD MULLAHS

I tried without success to get through that day without a drink. Persecutory, mind-racing turmoil and a powerful craving drove me to the empty suitcase in the wardrobe, then downstairs to the bottle, before I remembered that there was no alcohol left. Determined to stop, I had poured it all down the sink the night before. Bewildered, I burst into tears, crept back to my bedroom and dressed, ready to go to the off-licence as soon as it opened.

I chain-smoked and paced the room until, with a flash of demonic joy, I remembered the top of the wardrobe. I stood on a chair and feverishly scrambled among the empty bottles until I found a half bottle of Smirnoff vodka. I sat on a chair and drank it neat with slow deliberation, until three of the Horsemen faded, leaving the intractable fourth, the grey despair, which magnified with the last of the vodka. Alcohol was not working for me any more. I forced myself to telephone my old friend.

"Joe, I don't want to live."

"You don't want to die either, Brid. I'll ask Zofia to take you to a Sobriety meeting at once. Hilda Uphill is off on second honeymoon to Marrakesh, the gateway to the desert, with Albert."

"She is what?"

"I met Albert at a funeral. They left yesterday."

"I wouldn't ask her anyway. I'll call Zofia."

"Pour the alcohol down the sink and get to a meeting."

"It's all gone."

"Good girl. Call me when you come back."

Handling life felt as dangerous as handling nitroglycerine, and I envied Hilda who seemed to have scrambled out of trouble. I did as Joe told me. Sometimes he could get me to do what I did not want to do. Limbs shaking, I bathed, struggled into clothes and called Zofia. Had something awful happened? Not life or death dreadful, but I needed her now. She came at once, as she would, but thought I was over-reacting to a nasty hangover, nothing time and a few aspirins would not cure. When I told her the problem was serious and I needed her to come to a Sobriety meeting with me, she said I was crazy, and if I was not that far gone, the mad mullahs in Sobriety would drive me crazy. Nobody in Zofia's view should be asked to live in this world without alcohol. Even the Blessed Lord had turned water into wine. It was the fruit of the earth, the work of human hands and meant to gladden the hearts of men. I shouted at her to look up the nearest meeting and drive me there. My hands were too shaky and sweaty to hold the *Where To Find* booklet. As we walked to the car, Zofia wanted to know what Pan Barowski thought of all this, and hearing that I had not seen him for weeks, said she should be driving me to a lunatic asylum, not a boring meeting of sad drunks in a church hall to be brainwashed into living a teetotal life.

"What's the real problem?" she asked as she took the wheel.

"Stanley wants me back."

"Back where?"

"Back to Africa."

"Dog's blood. You are really off your head. What about Pan Barowski?"

"He is gone. I'm afraid to divorce and marry a Pole. I did wrong to get involved."

"You are a human being, for God's sake."

"Stanley needs me and Malachy. He has been very sick."

"Rubbish. He left you both. He's managed without either of you."

"Malachy needs his father."

"He needs him like a hole in the head. Anja and I and the baby will manage without the bloody father."

"Oh Zofia, if I could feel glad about anything it would be about that. What about the community?"

"To hell with the community. I bet you they'll come to the christening even if it's out of curiosity."

She pulled up outside the church hall, put her arm around my shoulder.

"We have a half-hour before the meeting starts. What makes you think it will work the second time around, darling? What about Malachy's education?"

"He could go to boarding school."

"He will end up a sado-masochistic kerb crawler."

"Oh Zofia, your English is improving."

"I read the papers."

"Malachy could stand it to see us together again."

"Never stay together for the children. Anja did not thank me. You will not be thanked."

"Look what the Polish people did to you, and you are one of them. What might they do to me?"

"Screw them. You saw me survive, and you have me as an ally in the Polish camp which is more than I had. Learn to control the drink, make a decision, Barowski will wait."

"He is furious. He may not wait."

"Risk it, and screw him if he doesn't."

In all the years that we had supported and loved one another, I had not heard such fighting talk from my friend. Zofia was coming on, and she did not call me Mrs Brid any more. Her marriage was not holding her back any more. Relationships could hold you back.

The meeting in a church hall in Hampstead was open to the public, and I tried to look as if I were attending for medical research or accompanying a real alcoholic, in case I were recognised. Dr Finucane's wife an alcoholic? No wonder he left her. Stiff-backed with pride and the humiliation of being forced to be with alcoholics at this hour of my life, I followed Zofia up the smoke-filled crowded hall to seats beside the top table. Could these be the alcoholics? There was not a blue nose or a dirty raincoat to be seen.

"When do they bring in the alcoholics?" I whispered to Zofia.

"These are the alcoholics," she said, hiding a giggle behind her hand.

I could hardly believe it. These people were well-dressed, laughing, chattering and smoking. Had nobody told them that cigarettes were carcinogenic? They must have a death wish.

The old feeling of worthlessness came up and I projected it, as I had always done, on my surroundings. Contempt of silly worthless people was easier to bear than my own lack of self-esteem. It was a well-worn defence. I read the slogans hanging on the walls. Sobriety is a Train; Put Down Your Baggage and Be Carried. A Meeting is Mind Dialysis. Let Go and Let God, If Sick and Tired of Being Sick and Tired. You Are Not Alone. Give Time Time. Three huge posters hanging behind the top table carried the twelve steps, twelve traditions and twelve promises.

They meant nothing to me. I hid my shaking hands under my handbag. What would Adam say if he could see me now, branded with the stigma of alcoholism? Any steps he might take would be long ones away from me.

When the meeting was opened by a raven-haired woman in shocking pink at the top table, I realised that Zofia was right. There was nobody else to be brought in. The chain-smoking cheerfully reckless people all around me were the alcoholics. I learned that they were learning to live one day at a time or sometimes one hour at a time without alcohol. That was the priority.

The woman in the shocking pink dress opened the meeting with a few minutes silence for the suffering alcoholics inside and outside the rooms. The traditions were read, of which I heard nothing except that principles came before personalities. Neither could I hear the twelve steps, except God was mentioned and practicing the principles in our affairs. The guest speaker, Charles by name, a heavy-shouldered man with clever eyes in a crinkly middle-aged face, would share his experience, strength and hope. We were invited to relax, to listen to the similarities, not the differences, and told that the newcomers were the most important people in the room.

Charles sounded like a Shakespearean actor, the sexy mellifluous voice piercing my alcoholic fog, reverberating around my befuddled mind. He had lost wives, homes, children. Alcohol gave him wings to fly, then removed the sky. Alcohol was a liquid bullet to the brain. He owed his life to the tough unconditional love of his sponsor, who told him that the head that brought him in would bring him out again, and that he must, the language was not his, "change, mother-fucker, or die". He was told to forget work, a habit has no pockets, to put down the drink and get to ninety meetings in ninety days.

The door to Sobriety swings both ways, and he left wanting to murder that man, ending up in the gutter looking down on what he saw as the God Squad, the Step Nazis, the fundamentalists in Sobriety. He was picked up out of the gutter by that sponsor, taken to a treatment centre, where they silenced the circus between his ears with a liquid medical cosh, taught him to eat, to walk the paraldehyde shuffle, to sleep without a cockroach army coming over the hill or a committee of vultures at the end of the bed every morning.

The sponsor, an ex-convict jailed for murdering his wife in a blackout, taught him he did not have to do life or feelings on his own and that the journey was an inside job. If the camel could begin and end the day on his knees, then so could he. When the murderous rage shifted, he was shocked to find unconditional love in its place for the ex-convict, something he had not experienced with parents, wives or children. Crying around the clock was another new experience. Today he knew that if he thought he were cured, the disease was doing press-ups getting ready to flatten him; or thought he were rid of his defects, they were regrouping for attack over the hill. He had the three most common factors in an alcoholics life—high sensitivity, a distant parent of the same sex and unresolved grief—and while he could never be cured, his alcoholism could be arrested. His story finished, a woman shared back her story of joyride to treadmill drinking. It was a tale of such creeping disaster and dicing with death that my notion of myself as the queen of tragedy was punctured. Stories were shared of childhood abuse, neglect, children killed in drunken car accidents, repetitive failed suicide attempts, even a beloved dog starved to death. I had those three factors Charles mentioned, but I did not think I was gone far enough to let Fred die like that.

"It's better than the theatre," Zofia whispered in my ear. "It's real life."

It was the first time in England that I was in a room full of people who professed or proposed to believe in a

God. People hoping to arrest an incurable disease, while killing themselves with cigarettes. People wrestling with a death wish. Strange people. I had once called the English bone-headed agriculturists in spiteful reprisal for oppressing my country, my language, my religion—my prejudice solidifying into self-evident truth. Contempt and prejudice. No wonder I drank. Yet the room was charged with the strong energy of hope. The meeting ended with the Serenity prayer lead by Charles the erstwhile atheist back from the dead. For acceptance of the unchangeable, for courage to change the changeable, and for the wisdom to know the difference, and to keep coming back without picking up the first drink.

What did they mean, accept the things I could not change? Was I to accept Barowski's storming out because he could not get his own way? Was I to accept Stanley back, the deserter of his son as well as his wife? I had no courage to change anything, or wisdom to know anything, but I was moved to be asked back. As we made our way out of the lively, smoky, crowded hall, I thought that if nobody else wanted me, at least these poor mad people did. I would consider coming back, even with all that was going on in my life. But I could not see my way not to pick up the first drink as soon as I got home.

Chapter Twenty-Four

SOBRIETY

The hope gained in the meeting was fragile, fleeting, draining out of me on the journey home. The jargon jingle spoken at the meeting was irritating and foreign to me, leaving me awash with alienation.

"You won't go wrong with those people," said Zofia. "I'll come to the meetings with you to start with."

"How come you called them mad mullahs this morning?" I asked.

"It's plain to see they are better without the drink," she said.

"This morning you thought that nobody should have to live without alcohol, the work of human hands and the fruit of the earth."

"The meeting has changed my mind," she said.

"Charles has changed your mind," I said with some savagery. "It's time you stopped fancying men younger than yourself."

Twisting the knife in the wound left by the young Jurek on Zofia was despicable.

"Forgive me," I said.

"Thousands would not, but I will. You are off your head," she said.

Inconsistent people were less dangerous than the rigidly consistent brigade I suspected I had just witnessed in action. Censorially, I judged the meeting to be far from therapeutic, with the talk of doing life like penal servitude, of enduring life instead of enjoying it. If that were the case, those poor people might as well drink until it killed them, and so might I, even if alcoholism was a virulently slow road to the graveyard. The prospect of becoming a wet-brained vegetable in nappies was too awful and I refused to contemplate it. London looked drab, toxic, the people haggard, dreary, the streets dismal and dim as the day stole out, dragging the light behind it, letting in the dusk with its lengthening shadows. The world was intolerable. I determined to drink into oblivion as soon as I got home. I remembered there was a bottle of vodka under the ball cock in the lavatory tank.

Zofia had other ideas. She was waiting for me as I came out of the lavatory, defiantly clutching the bottle behind my back. She grabbed the bottle and won the ensuing wrestling match, her physical strength a match for my maniacal determination. I sank to my knees in angry tears as she emptied the bottle down the lavatory bowl. She sat beside me on the carpet, then manoeuvered me into bed and forced me to take sleeping pills and camomile tea. Whose side was she on, I shouted at her?

The sleeping pills began to work, and I remembered the mad mullahs saying I would have to change if I wanted to stop drinking and get what they had. Whatever it was they had was certainly better than what I had. I had a washing machine going around at top speed in my head. They had said I would have to change or die. Change what? How could I change myself when I did not know who or what I was? I could not change the men who were bent on getting their own way, and how could I accept that? All of that process might be necessary for real alcoholics but not for me. It was me and them. I was different. A special case. The most normal of persons given the same unjust treatment in life would have drunk like me. Filled with self-justification, I began to drift into drugged oblivion, wondering whether Charles was the star of theatre, films or television. Innocent of all that lay before me, I lost consciousness.

"Deus ex machina," I heard myself shout, as I awoke from a celestial dream the next morning. Yet I found that if God had come out of the works for me to solve the unsolvable in the nick of time, He had botched it. The craving for alcohol at the back of my throat was worse than ever. So much for divine intervention. I gulped the contents of the Coca-Cola bottle left by Zofia the night before. I did not want to get up and face the world without alcohol. Eat chocolate to replace the sugar intake and reduce the craving, they had said. I ravenously ate a Mars chocolate bar I found in Malachy's room, and after a few minutes the craving did leave me. There was some truth in what they said then.

I read some of the literature. I was to watch out for

H.A.L.T.: hungry, angry, lonely and tired. I was all of the four. I ate cornflakes, lay on the floor, heart-sore through repeated replay of John McCormack's wrenching Irish love songs, in mourning for the loss of love in my life, until I was no longer hungry, angry, lonely or even too tired. The mad mullahs had been through it. They knew something, while I did not know how to live with alcohol or without it.

I found a medical book of Stanley's on the concept of alcoholism as a disease. If I had to admit to alcoholism, then I'd prefer to be sick rather than immoral. The brain chemistry of the alcoholic could take five years in sobriety to return to normal. Maybe it was hypothetical, but there must be something in it. On the back page it said that the World Health Service pronounced alcoholism an illness, and that was good enough for me until they pronounced the opposite. If I was one of them I was a sick woman and everybody better be nice to me.

Galvanised with self-pity and self-righteousness, I read the Twelve Promises, to see if it would be worth my while to stop drinking. I could expect freedom, happiness, serenity and peace, and a changed attitude to the world. I would come to realise that God was doing for me what I could not do for myself. What if there were no God? What if there were? The promises were not extravagant and would materialise if I worked for them. In a harsh moment of clarity I saw that Sobriety was my only hope. There was no alternative, because I had reached what they called the jumping off place.

I rang Lydia, and she came at once. I went downstairs to let her in.

"Brid, is there anything wrong? My God, what's happened?"

"Lydia, I'm an alcoholic. Zofia took me to Sobriety."

"Have you stopped drinking?"

"I don't know. I don't know if I can."

"Yes, you can. If others can do it, you can do it. You must go to the meetings. I'll come with you."

"Zofia has more time than you have. At least until Anja's baby comes."

"Malachy and Disraeli are worried about your drinking."

"Oh God, how do you know that?"

"They told Tom. We didn't like to tell you with all you've gone through. Will you reconcile with Stanley?"

"I have no idea."

"Look after yourself now. When is Malachy back from camp?"

"In a week."

"Right. You have a week. You won't know yourself in a week. I don't have to tell you that Tom and I are here for you."

I burst into tears and she held me until I stopped.

It was difficult enough for me to count to ninety meetings in ninety days, never mind attend them, but I set out to do it. I was looking better, if not feeling better, when Malachy arrived back from camp.

"You look different, Mimmo," he said after we hugged and kissed.

"So do you," I said.

"I have a girlfriend, Mom. Her name is Becky and she wants to marry me when we are old enough."

"Sensible girl. How do I look different?"

"Your eyes is shiny."

"I've stopped drinking, Malachy."

"For good?"

"For good. I've joined Sobriety."

"What's Sobriety?"

"A fellowship of sober people."

"Where is Pan Barowski?"

"Gone."

"For good?"

"I don't know."

"I liked him a lot."

"I thought you disliked him."

"I was being childish about you and Daddy."

My God, Zofia was right. Building one's life for children was crazy. Becky had driven Africa and Stanley out of his head.

Live in the day, the members of Sobriety said. An eye on both the past and the future would leave me swivel-headed, cross-eyed, confused. An alcoholic was like a stagnant lake without an inlet. I was told to learn to listen, listen to learn, and share my feelings at every meeting. Rage and jealousy seen in others was the signal to look at myself and take my projections back. If you spot it, you've got it, they said. I was not to make a decision about my life until the alcoholic fog lifted. I would find out how to change and what to change by doing the steps. I would have to take the steps to get well and not wait to get well to do them. Bring the body, they said, and the head will follow.

Chapter Twenty-Five

WALKING THE WALK

I risked asking Thelma, the lady of the daring pink dress, to be my sponsor. Her smiling face, with its deeply indented frown line and a network of fine ones, carried the legacy of a life lived on the edge. Detecting that the raven hair was dyed, the bold teeth tobacco stained, the back of her hands showing the brown liver spots of advancing old age gave me the courage. If I were prepared to go to any lengths, she would take me through the steps. I was to clean house and let God in. He did not like vacuums.

"I have no God," I said.

"You will find one," she smiled.

"How?" I asked.

"By doing what I tell you. Do you pray in the morning?"

"I don't believe in prayer."

"Tomorrow, you will get down on your hands and knees and turn your life and your will over to a Higher Power for the day."

"I cannot. It is dishonest."

"Throw your shoes under the bed tonight, and when you kneel on one knee to find them, bend the other."

"How can I hand my life and my will to a power I don't believe in?"

"How did you get here?"

"The 37 bus."

"Hand it over to the power of the bus. Fake it to make it. It works."

I did it, but not to the bus. I did it to the energy I felt at the meetings.

I didn't want her to be right, but she was. The compulsion to drink was lifted. The savage state of my mind lessened enough for me to learn that I must put aside my contempt and my lack of faith, and investigate. I must put aside the futility of my existence and investigate. I must change my point of view. Sobriety was doing for me what nothing or nobody else could have done.

"The express elevator to sobriety don't work, ducky," said Thelma. "We take the steps one at a time."

"The rest of my life?" I quavered.

"Reversin' stinkin' thinkin' and emotional potty-training takes time."

"Potty-training?"

"Emotional potty-training. Child abuse and alcohol abuse stunt growth. Unresolved grief is a bugger. We have to grow up or continue to throw up."

Unresolved grief. I began to see that it had held me back

all my adult life. Afraid to take a risk. Afraid all my life to love any man. Afraid I'd have to go through it all again. I had foolishly thought it might be safe with someone as young as Malachy. But he was as old now as Shane had been. Life was terminal. I began to tremble. I would have to do what Thelma told me to do whether I liked it or not.

She showed me around the titillating room got up like a seashore cave where we were to begin work on the Twelve Steps. A glass tank filled with wonders in sea water stood under white muslin curtains billowing like wave crests at an open window. Sea horses and red-spotted anemones floated over a pink miniature coral reef. I focused on a transparent jelly fish, an orange starfish and a violet-shelled snail to calm my thoughts. The furthest end of the room was like a shingle beach, with baskets of stones, pebbles and a variety of sea shells. Dead wood logs hung starkly artistic on a wall, and a kitchen sink filled with plants stood in a corner. Glacial apprehension gripped me to be taking an intimate journey with a woman who had to live in a sea cave to rest her head. We sat with mugs of coffee near the tank.

"Step one. Are you clear you cannot manage alcohol or your life?"

"I cannot be clear. I have a problem with two men."

"Living rent free in your head no doubt. Who are they?"

"My husband in Africa and my lover in London."

"Which one made you happiest in bed?"

"I hadn't thought about it."

"Think about it."

"The lover, I suppose."

"The body don't lie. Are you handing over your life to a Higher Power every morning?"

"Some mornings."

"Every morning if you want results."

I wanted results. I watched the dead eyes of wretched newcomers like myself, with the light out and nobody home in the heads, come to life, so I did as I was told, living robotically one day at a time. Recovery from such soul sickness was contingent on my spiritual condition they said. It was not a religious programme, a race, a competition, or a menu where I could pick and choose. I was to start at the beginning.

Zofia had been right about never building your life for children, and if Thelma was right and the body did not lie, I was a fool to let Adam go. Sourly, I thought that the body would lie if it could lie. My body had drawn comparisons between Stanley and Adam when I could not. Could I call Adam, try to get him back? I could not. Not until I could swallow my pride and risk rejection. I was told that rejection could be God's protection, and if I could come to see it like that I would not be so fearful of it. I was told to make no major decisions until the alcoholic fog lifted and the brain chemistry returned to normal. They told me I need never drink again, and I came to believe them. The Power was working and it was not from the 37 bus.

If Joe could get enough energy to heal Malachy, maybe I could get some too. I had suspected him of making it up, trying to convert me. Contempt prior to investigation was a stumbling block I could no longer afford.

"Get the worst out first," said Thelma cheerfully.

The compulsion to strangle her was overwhelming. "Get the worst out first" rang in my head for months, as I wrote and cried, cried and wrote, until it was done. The jargon penetrated the fog and smashed the class barriers. Resentments bred when my instincts for sex, security, social life were threatened had to be written down. I was to put aside the wrongs, imagined or real, done to me, and look for my own mistakes, if I wanted liberty. She read what I had written with care, said that she had done in spades what I had done in clubs, told me to tear it up.

"Let your brother go. Let him rest in peace, and move on."

"I don't know how."

"Write to him daily for a month. Visit his grave and say goodbye."

"It's in Ireland."

"Do it. Walk through the grief and get well. Share it and Sobriety will carry you."

"I have the seven deadly sins," I said.

"Join the club. Practise the opposite. Act as if you had humility, charity, honesty. And while you're at it, practise patience and tolerance with the head bangers in Sobriety."

"I cannot do it."

"You have to. There's no cure. Stick with the travellers on the journey and avoid the bleeding deacons like Patrick the Pope and Hellfire Harry, who think they have arrived. Avoid the fundamentalist God Squad at the Joys of Recovery meetings and elsewhere. You can tell the buggers by the fixed smile on their faces."

I did what she told me insofar as I was able, went through the pain which passed without killing me, and gradually the feeling of impending doom faded. I had to stop doing what I wanted to do, had always done. I had to begin to do what I did not want to do, had never done.

"I have not the strength."

"Spot on, ducky. Like millions before you, you have to turn to a Higher Power."

"A Higher Power is incomprehensible to my intellect."

"And to the rest of the human race. Get a concept, get experience. The hole inside every alcoholic is God-shaped. Nothing else will fill it. Progress not perfection, Brid. We are not saints."

Thelma looked nothing like a saint. The nails on her hands and feet matched the blood red lipstick, and her shorts were short indeed. My Thelma of the coruscating wit and crazy lifestyle. She drove me through the Steps as, savagely and reluctantly, I made lists and amends to the people I had harmed. I fought with her over them, for I felt the world owed me the apology. She told me that I was shutting out what didn't suit me. Defiance, rage and rebellion kept me in thrall for weeks, until the discomfort drove me to wanting a drink, and fear drove me to surrender.

I was to pray for and forgive my mother Mary Rafferty and own my part in the estrangement.

"She destroyed my life. I cannot forgive her."

"Did she intend to damage you?"

"How the hell do I know? I was a child."

"What were her parents like?"

"She never spoke of them."

"Did you never ask her?"

"No. They were dead before I was born."

"Did it not occur to you that she was probably damaged herself and did the best she could with what she had?"

"No."

"Share it at every meeting."

"I can't do that in public."

"You are as sick as your secrets. Keep them and you will drink again."

"Change or die." Charles had said that at my first meeting. The courage came from listening to the people. I swallowed my huge pride. I ranted, raved, wept, for weeks and then months, about the hostility, the humiliation perpetrated on me as a child. I walked around with what I called my canister of grief and dread contained in my chest for month after month, and Thelma was right; it did not kill me. People listened without complaint and came to show kindness afterwards. I was understood. I began to feel a little better, a little lighter, as the burden began to dissolve.

"Are you willing to become willing to make a decision about your husband in the African bush and the gentleman here, and to make amends to them both?" asked Thelma, six months after we had begun the sessions.

"I can see I must decide which one to let into my life. That is if I decide to let either of them into my life, but what do you mean make amends to them for God's sake? Amends for what?

"Think about it. It's not a race."

I thought about it as the weeks passed by and the more I did so the more confused and insane I became. I took my angst to Thelma.

"All will be revealed to you in time about your choice of partner," she consoled me. "But you must not delay about making amends. Delay is dangerous. Pray for the courage and the honesty."

"I have failed to see why I need to make amends to either Stanley or Adam Barkowski," I said.

"Did you or did you not take their peace from them?"

"I never set out to take their peace from them. And how do I know whether they had any peace before they met me? Look at the way they both treated me."

"We are trying to deal with your behaviour, not theirs. You have a killer illness and your recovery is contingent on your spiritual condition. You have a full time job dealing with your stuff. If you want to get well, ducky, you are going to have to do it. Think about it."

"I don't see why I should make amends to either of them."

"Think about it until you do see."

"I'll think about it tomorrow." I said as I had always done.

"You will think about it today," said my Thelma.

Chapter Twenty-Six

SILENCE IN THE HEAD

It took months before I could focus on my dilemma without bringing on a panic attack. Was any man worth being in such a state? Were either of the two men in question worth it? When all was said and done, what was there to choose between them? One of them had piercing grey eyes, the other had flashing dark ones, and while both were fine figures of manhood, neither of them were in the first flush of youth. Neither of them had led easy lives. Either of them or both of them could be defunct any minute now from a heart attack, and here I was attempting to decipher at which pair of feet I would lay my heart and my life. If I did as Stanley wanted, Malachy and I must emigrate to Wad Medani. While Stanley as an experienced physician might try his best to help me recover from alcoholism, my life would have to be managed without Sobriety's design and support for living, for alcoholism was probably swept under the carpet by Sharia law in Wad Medani.

Thelma said I must learn to be a human being instead of a human doing, trying to run before I could walk. I must learn reliance not defiance, and allow the slow process of uncovery, discovery and recovery to take place. The jargon was a two-edged sword, cutting across the class divide, carrying truth and humour. Gradually, as I had been promised it would, the alcoholic fog lifted and I was able to think about thinking what to do with the rest of my life without having a panic attack. While it could take up to five years for the brain chemistry to return to normal, I must deal with life as best I could by practising the principles in all my affairs. While I gave Thelma the credit for hammering home the imaginative message on building a strong spiritual home with humility, charity and honesty, I could not remember what the other principles were. I recognised however that I must put out of my life anything that might drive me to drink. Or anybody. The trouble was that without the drink, I was like a crustless crustacean, afraid even of poor Mr Pocock, who seemed to have no friends and who did nothing more offensive to me than play romantic music on his piano.

"I'm frightened of my neighbour Walter Pocock," I said. "He's a lonely man."

"Is he bothering you?"

"He has taken to playing romantic music since Stanley left. I can hear him through the walls."

"Is he keeping you awake at night?"

"No."

"Leave him alone. You cannot fix anyone's loneliness but your own. If he gets nasty, there are men in the fellowship to deal with that."

I was learning to ask for help, and the wonder was that I was getting it. Fear was a coward, they said. Faced it runs away. F.E.A.R. given in to meant "fuck, everything, and run" they said. The unaccustomed silence in my head was disconcerting, but Thelma said the quiet in my mind was a signal that I had done the right thing. Right things would happen if I did the right things. Thelma was right. You had to clean house, to clean your side of the street to get well. Paranoia had to go.

I had to pray for the soul of Mary Rafferty who had not willfully intended to damage me, even if she did get satisfaction from projecting her venom on to me. Projecting the venom gave her a rest from it, and she needed that rest. She was a human being after all. I was to work to understand the woman, and forgiveness would follow. I learned that I was a victim of a victim who had done the best she could, and while it was not good enough, I would get nowhere without charity. It was a very slow transition from my harsh internalised image of Mary Rafferty to that of a stoical hard-working mother whose own sick mother had given her away to a mean spinster aunt. Who was I to judge the mother who had no father to protect her, while I had a father like John Rafferty? It was an inside job, slow and painful. No gain without pain, they said. Get out the anger or it comes out sideways in nasty ways like sarcasm, contempt and bitterness, they said.

It became time for me to work towards a decision about Stanley and Adam Barowski, to face the harm I had done them. How was I going to swallow my pride and admit anything to them? I was told to swallow it or it would kill me.

I tried to face the fact that I had probably married Stanley for the wrong reasons. The young Stanley was handsome, a good dancer, but would I have looked at him without the glittering career ahead of him? I would not. That was the truth. Had I married for money then? I would never have admitted to it. I would have defended my right to security, my right to a glamorous fun-filled life, would have denied the fact that I married him in case somebody else did. Had I ever stopped for one moment in the dash to the races, the parties and the pubs to consider Stanley's needs, what I had to give him, or whether I loved him at all? If I had, I could not remember it. While drinking, I would have protested that there had been no time, we had been too young to know what love was, but sober, I could not get away with denial any more. I would have to write to Stanley. And tell him what? The drinking Brid, so terrified of abandonment in a hostile world, would have checked out whether Adam Barowski was available first. A further change, nearly imperceptible to me, must be taking place. Be all that as it may, what was I going to say to Stanley? It was hardly making amends to say, "I married you with my head and not my heart." Then I remembered that Stanley didn't need me to tell him that. He had known the truth long before and finally been driven to walk away from it. What could have changed his mind? Could it be that he was suffering from loneliness among the smiling people in the Nile town? Was it that he wanted to have his son with him and, when it came to me, that the devil you knew was better than the devil you didn't. The low self-esteem of the alcoholic stifled any belief that he might still love me and was hoping for change. Yet I remembered that there had been a moment as we sat in the green light under a canopy of trees, watching the silver moon track on the river Nile, that the energy between us was tangible, and the time of goodbye at the airport filled with sadness in spite of my anger at the thought we might never see one another again.

Yet what did that signify, when in all the years we had spent together, my heart had never somersaulted, I had never gone weak at the knees at the sight of him, nor had I ever been swept up to a high place of peace while sharing his bed. The body didn't know how to lie, Thelma had said. I came to see that I would have to let Stanley go, for I saw with hurtful clarity that he deserved more than I ever had to give him and might find it, once shot of me. I owed him that if I was ever to make amends, and maybe one day we might sit together with Malachy beside the Nile. Nobody was going to take that hope away from me. Not even Adam Barowski.

I decided not to tell Malachy until the Christmas holidays. Whether that was out of prudence or procrastination, I could not tell at first until I found I was afraid to approach either Stanley or himself. I would have to find the courage to follow one of the first principles of Sobriety, to change the things I could. Thelma ordered me to walk through the fear and do it. I was beginning to trust her. I did what she told me to do.

Dear Stanley, I wrote,
> *I have thought long and with as much honesty as I can muster, and that as you know is hard for me to do. I have thought about your invitation to share the rest of your life, and I have come to a conclusion, which would cause me untold grief if I did not cling to the hope that we can be together with Malachy from time to time. I have faced the fact that I do not have it in me to give you what you deserve in a wife, that I never had it, and that I married you for selfish reasons and without due thought or care for your needs. I see that you were right to leave me and I can understand even while I cannot condone how you did it. I am a recovering alcoholic attempting to live the only way open to the likes of me, a spiritual life in Sobriety, and I have all the emotional sickness of such people, but then nobody knows that better then you. I am sorry for the grief I caused you then and for any I cause you now, but it didn't work before and it cost you. I hope we may be friends. I don't know the outcome of any relationship with Barowski, as I have not seen him for months. I am learning to live one day at a time. Malachy is nearly as tall as you are, his school reports are fine and he has a girlfriend called Becky. Write to him. I will tell*

him of my decision now. I respect and admire
you, and for the work you are doing in Wad
Medani. I am proud to know you. I was never
worth your little finger. Look after yourself.
Write.

Love, Brid.

I posted the letter before I could change my mind and
spent an uneasy night of stinkin' thinkin', wondering if
I had not been over the top in eating such humble pie,
for when all was said and done, he had buggered off
without a thought of the consequences for Malachy,
never mind me. However, the profound silence in the
head was back next day, so I knew that I had acted cor-
rectly. Charity paid off.

"Daddy and I will remain friends Malachy. You and I
will visit him in Africa, but we will not reconcile as man
and wife."

Malachy marked his place in his physics book.

"OK, Mom. It's no surprise really, and not so awful if
we can be together sometimes . . . if I can get to see
Daddy soon."

"You are old enough to fly by yourself, after your
exams."

"Oh gosh, Mom, better tell Daddy I'm coming. And
better eat vitamins, Mom. You got pale lately."

It was as easy as that, with neither of us mentioning
Adam Barowski, and the silence in my head remained all
evening.

Chapter Twenty-Seven

ONE IN THE HAND

"Have you decided that one man in the hand is worth one in the bush?" asked Thelma.

"In a manner of speaking, I have."

I lay awake at night wondering how and when I should approach Adam. Supposing he had found someone else, a woman who could fit into the community, who was familiar with the language and the cuisine. A Polish woman. My spirit drooped at the thought of being replaced, and my mind raced with the terror of abandonment. Thelma told me to calm down, to do the foot work and find out the unidealised facts of the case. Rejection was often God's protection, she said. Alcoholics were disappointed idealists, and I was to avoid more of that. I pocketed my pride and telephoned Zofia for help.

"Will you help me, Zofia?"

"If I can."

"Can you find out if Pan Barowski is free?"

"What do you mean, free?"

"If he's found a more suitable woman or not."

"Jesu Maria, can you not ask him yourself?"

"I'm afraid."

"What do you mean a more suitable woman?"

"Someone who can speak the language and cook the Polish way."

"It wasn't your language or your cooking he was interested in."

"Zofia, I need to find out if he's no longer interested."

"I can only try to find out if there is another woman. Give me an hour, and I'll call back."

And sure enough, she rang back within the hour. A testimony to the efficacy and speed of communication in her community. All must be well now between her and them. The expected baby had made the difference perhaps.

"Hi, Brid. You are in with a chance, as far as my gossip-mongers can tell, but he is a popular man with the ladies. I take it you're not going to Africa then?"

"No, not for good."

"Bravo. Stick with Sobriety now. It's clearing your head."

"Thanks. What do they mean he is popular with the ladies?"

"Women like him, and you might as well know that before as after. Goodbye now and good luck."

I felt faint. A popular man with the ladies. Was Zofia warning me? How could I expect to be happy, joyous and free, like the promises said, with a man who was popular with the ladies? Others might, but I was too insecure. I went into the sitting room, sat beside the window. A skittish wind drove swollen, rain-laden clouds across the church spire on the hill. Sadly, I remembered John Rafferty standing outside the kitchen door with his head raised, smelling rain on the wind long before the downpour. I opened the window. Yes, it wouldn't be long now. I was not my father's daughter for nothing.

Now that autumn had closed in on the garden, the brown bark of the hawthorn tree was flaky, the clusters of white flowers, so dense among the leaves on the thorny boughs, were shed on the grass. Only the purple haws, unstripped yet by the birds, remained. Rufous-breasted swallows with long forked tails congregated on the telegraph wires, preparing to migrate to Africa for the winter. Where Stanley was.

I wondered what he was doing just then, felt silent unresolved grief churn my stomach until I remembered Thelma ordering me to focus on the answer not the problem. The answer to the self-inflicted confusion in my life. I was unravelling that. The answer to what? To the loneliness of the single life? Many a marriage was worse. To the distant mothering, the isolation imposed upon myself after Shane's death.

The unconditional love in Sobriety was the answer if I stayed and worked the steps. Did I think Adam Barowski could fix me? If it works don't fix it, Thelma said. Sobriety worked. I had seen it. I did not need Adam to fix me. What did I need him for? To risk life again? To risk love again, for life was scabrous without love. Was I being drawn back like a dog to its vomit, to take the risk of feeling the same kind of pain which had stilled and chilled my development long years ago? The kind of love you could neither live with nor without, like the alcohol I had not been able to live with or without. I must be mad. I trembled at the thought of some other woman in his life. I should be able to wish for his happiness with or without me, but I was no saint; such altruism was way beyond me.

The back door closed with a bang, and Fred barked joyously as there came running steps and a knock on the sitting room door.

"Come in," I called.

"It's me, Mrs Finucane. Where's Malachy please?"

Disraeli was dressed in his white cricket clothes. I braced myself as Fred hurtled on to my lap as he had done when a puppy. I held the barrel-shaped furry body, then shoved him off.

"He's in his room. Up you go."

"Africa is only for visiting."

"Oh?"

"Yes. You have to have a black skin for Africa or you can get cancer. There are dangerous snakes and black buffalo. So Lydia and Tom and me think you better not go there. And it's too far away from us."

As he went out, I felt grateful that I would see Disraeli grow up. And what about Fred, now lying on my feet? The climate in Wad Medani would have killed him. He panted with the heat, his tongue hanging out over his jaws, in mild summer days. Fred, smelling at both ends sometimes, with fleas most of the time, had showed me unconditional love, and I could not have left him behind.

As the sky darkened I watched a brace of fast-flying bronze backed turtle doves alight on a thorny branch outside the window. I could hear the far-carrying purring call through the window, as I had heard it in my childhood running in the woods. In flight to the scrub, the woodland or the farms to the north no doubt. Dejectedly, I watched them take off too soon and fly away high above the trees and out of sight. "Arise my love and come, the voice of the turtle dove is heard in the land." My lover had not called me. If he had loved me, he would have fought to prevent me going to Africa. Had he not come within an ace of losing me to Stanley? The phrase "very popular with the ladies" hummed around the circuit of my racing mind. Zofia warning me that if I didn't get him somebody else would? Was not that the reason I had hijacked Stanley? In case somebody else got him. I was not going to get a chance to ruin Adam's life as I had Stanley's for he wouldn't let me. Nobody was going to hijack the likes of Adam Barowski. He was a much harder nut to crack than the young Stanley Finucane. I need only be responsible for my own motivation, and I would have to see him first to find out what the truth of that was.

There was more to life than somersaulting hearts and weak knees. All I had to find out was what he wanted, and I had no control over that. I accepted that he was not going to come to me no matter how long I waited. He had waited for me to come back from Africa to him, and I had failed him. He would have thought that if I had loved him, I could not have turned him away. But had I turned him away? Had I not just asked for time after my journey? Now I could see that it would be all the same to him. There were no half measures with Adam Barowski. I would have to go to him, and it was as well that I had the support of Sobriety, for I could not face the possibility of rejection by myself, whether it was God's protection or not. Neither could I face humiliation by myself.

Better not give him an excuse to postpone a meeting by telephoning first. I would go to Polonia and face him in his den. What to wear? A purple tweed suit to hold me in one piece and to look as if I meant business. It was best to be matter of fact. Dressed in low-heeled shoes and handbag to match, I checked myself in the mirror, pulling leather gloves over shaking hands. I desperately wanted a drink to give me courage, to stop the shaking, but I knew that the first drink did the damage, and I could not risk it. My enzymes wouldn't break down the alcohol and I would be left with the craving.

Supposing he wasn't there and the train journey was for nothing? So what. I could try again tomorrow. Despite a fibrillating heart, I was beginning to believe that the journey in traversing the truth in the fellowship of Sobriety would help to clear the rubbish, the emptiness, and fill the hole inside me. Fulfilment was an inside job. I would not be asking Adam to fix me. I would be asking for permission to risk the pain of loving once more.

I walked from the station through the crowded wet streets to the Polonia. A sharp wind stripped the yellowing leaves off the trees, tossing them willy-nilly. Nobody took any notice of me as I walked through the bustling restaurant, down the corridor and knocked on the office door. The deep voice bidding me to come in was his. I took a breath and went in.

He wore the same lavender shirt I had first seen him in, and the circles under his eyes were black. He looked up from behind the pile of papers on his desk, and my knees dissolved at the expression of surprise, then gladness on his face. Words failed me as I closed the door and stood with my back to it for support. If he'd have me, I'd go Polish. He was worth it. He would always need to dance the polka with his eyes shut. We could pull up a drawbridge and keep the world out some of the time, and I could be the lady from the Emerald Isle. He got up from behind the desk.

"You are a sight for sore eyes, Miss Finucane," he said quietly, and held his arms out to me.

We sat on the floor with arms entwined until the blackness of night rolled the daylight up like a scroll and cast it out of the London sky.